DEATH ON DORADO

When wealthy businessman Edlin Borrowitch is murdered, Tec Sarn Denson is called in to defend the woman accused of the killing, Ros Kernwell. The case is a puzzling one and Denson finds her innocence difficult to prove. However, the one thing he doesn't lack is a list of suspects — but when everyone has a motive for murder, how can he choose? And how can he stay alive when the murderer is out to get him too?

JOHN LIGHT

DEATH ON DORADO

Complete and Unabridged

LINFORD
Leicester

First published in Great Britain

First Linford Edition
published 2009

British Library CIP Data

Light, John
    Death on Dorado.—Large print ed.—
Linford mystery library
1. Murder—Investigation—Fiction
2. Detective and mystery stories
3. Large type books
I. Title
823.9'12 [F]

ISBN 978–1–84782–600–8

Published by
F. A. Thorpe (Publishing)
Anstey, Leicestershire

Set by Words & Graphics Ltd.
Anstey, Leicestershire
Printed and bound in Great Britain by
T. J. International Ltd., Padstow, Cornwall

This book is printed on acid-free paper

1

Death of a Bizman

Sarn Denson hovered high above the silver sea. It was a beautiful dawn, and the distant city gleamed in the bright yellow of Aurum, so that the spires and towers were gold, and the shore outshone the sea. Beneath him, the silver, beyond the gold, and around and above, the deep cloudless blue of Dorado's crystal sky.

Tired though he was, Denson found the sight irresistible. His cruiser hung motionless while he gazed upon the scene. At the press of a button, the transparent canopy slid back, and the cool, pure air of morning washed over him, soothing the smart in his eyes, smoothing the frown from his face, and washing the smell of corruption from his nostrils.

It had been a long and bitter night, and the depths of depravity, which his investigations into the crimes of Kerent had revealed, had shaken even Denson's cynical acceptance of human perversion. He felt the need for a respite, for solitude in the presence of beauty, to remind him that there was goodness and enjoyment in life as well as evil and suffering.

Denson soon tired of goodness and beauty, and resumed his journey towards Gold City. He crossed the shoreline and sped between the sky-scraping towers. There was little traffic in the air — the city lived late into the night, and always seemed reluctant to greet the dawn.

Around him, the towers of gold rose sheer into the morning sky. They weren't pure gold, of course, since gold hasn't the mechanical strength necessary for construction work — it needs reinforcing with precious synthetics. Still, it looked just like ordinary gold; the valuable materials weren't exposed at the surface.

Denson approached his own building, a slender golden column like the stem of a gigantic plant, from which branched the berthing arms with their office nodules. Before docking, he checked his office on the viewscreen. The room wasn't a place for working, it was just somewhere for clients to leave messages, or, if they were desperate, wait. There was someone waiting now.

Denson looked her over carefully. She was young, not yet thirty standard years, he would guess, and good looking seen by herself. He doubted whether he'd notice her in a crowd, though. She seemed calm, yet she was waiting there for him. Something must be very wrong, he thought, for her to exercise such tight control when apparently unobserved.

Denson was a successful Tec, in the sense that he got results, but he worked alone and the rich contracts seldom came his way — they went to the big agencies where teamwork and sledgehammer thinking prevailed. Denson didn't like that style of working. Still, as long as he could afford to run his cruiser and keep up the payments on the office berth, and visit Goldenhaze occasionally, and get drunk from time to time, and . . .

Denson sighed. He didn't earn enough money even for his modest pleasures. It was time to get tough. No more philanthropic assignments.

The Tec nosed his cruiser into place. The lock below the pilot cabin closed with the port of the building nodule. At this early hour, there were few empty berths, and the building looked almost solid, so closely packed were the craft which surrounded him.

Sarn Denson, pale of countenance, hair brown and curly, eyes a tired grey, slight of build, but of medium height, rose and left the flight cabin. He descended to the lower deck and walked through his living quarters and his real office to the door which now communicated with his waiting room.

The woman started slightly as Denson came in. She looked up at him and he noted the wide blue eyes in an almost white face, framed by jet black hair. Her mouth was small and sombre. She rose awkwardly, as though she had been sitting motionless for a long time, and extended a slim, ringless hand. Denson took it, and it was cold against his own warm skin.

'Sorry if you've been waiting long,' he

said. He felt her eyes on him, noting the crumpled clothing and dirty face, and sensed her thoughts. He smiled crookedly. 'I'm just back from an all-night assignment. Haven't had time to clean up yet.'

'Of course,' she acknowledged, and her voice was slight, but tense.

'Well,' continued Denson, 'you came to see me and here I am, so what's the problem?'

He went and sat on the edge of his desk. The woman resumed her seat.

'You are Tec Denson?' she inquired. 'Tec Sarn Denson?'

Denson sighed. This looked like being a difficult one.

'For certain I am,' he replied, and handed her the identification card issued by the Tec Guild. She nodded, without looking at it. Denson could see she was doing things her training — whatever that was — had taught her, but mechanically, without commitment.

'So what's the problem?' he repeated.

'I understand you aren't expensive . . . ' she said, ignoring his question.

Denson contained his exasperation. 'I don't have a lot of fancy gadgets, and I work alone, so I don't have the overheads the bigger outfits have. But I do need to eat and drink, and run a cruiser, and rent this place. It all costs.'

Again she nodded, but without seeming to have listened to his reply.

Suddenly she whispered: 'I'm frightened!'

At last, thought the Tec, I'm going to find out what all this is about. He left the desk and sat closer to her, on a chair.

'Who's frightening you?' he probed gently.

'City Investigators Limited,' she replied.

Denson was taken aback. 'But they don't frighten people! Not law-abiding citizens, that is. They're respectable Tecs.'

The woman looked down, and when she spoke he could hardly hear her: 'They frighten me. They think I murdered my employer.'

'Did you?' asked Denson.

'Certainly not!' she retorted, and there was defiance in her eyes as she looked up again.

'You want me to prove it?' asked Denson rhetorically.

The woman nodded. 'Will you do it?' she pleaded. 'I'm not rich. I can't afford a large fee. Most of my earnings have gone into paying off the loan which financed my education. The Philanthropic Trust won't award grants for commercial studies.'

Inwardly Denson groaned. It looked like another case in which he'd be lucky if he broke even, let alone made a profit. He ought to shake his head and suggest she go somewhere else, but he knew he wouldn't. He'd give his all, whether he got the rate for the job or not.

'I'll do what I can for the money,' he said out loud. 'When it runs out, I'm finished. Want me on those terms?'

The woman's lip trembled at this financially brutal attitude, but she nodded her agreement.

'You'd better tell me the whole story,' commanded the Tec, 'starting with your name, which you forgot to tell me when we introduced ourselves.'

Ros Kernwell was an accountant. She

had graduated from Dorado's National Business College with honours in Visual Arts Accounting. She'd served some years in the First Gold City Bank as a Paintings Auditor, and had then gone to work for Edlin Borrowitch, one of Gold City's wealthiest and most successful business men. Now Bizman Borrowitch had been found dead.

'The Bizman had an enormous life insurance policy,' finished Ros Kernwell, 'and of course the company, Aurum Life, will want to keep the cost of investigating his death to a minimum. So City Investigators are under pressure to find a culprit, and they've picked on me.'

'How did Borrowitch die?' asked Denson.

'Poison,' replied Ros. 'It was one of those random action poisons which may cause death after a matter of hours, or not for weeks, so there's no way of knowing when it was administered.'

'So it's not much use seeing who had the opportunity — almost anyone might have. They'll have to concentrate on motive. Had you a reason for wanting the Bizman dead?'

'No,' said Ros quickly, 'but . . . '

'Then why are you worried?' interrupted the Tec irritably.

'Because it looks as though I had . . . ' finished the woman miserably.

With an effort, Denson pulled himself together. He was going about this consultation all wrong. People came to him because they were in trouble. They needed sympathy and understanding. He had no business bullying a client.

He smiled, and said in a voice as sympathetic as he could contrive: 'Tell me why anyone should think you wanted Bizman Borrowitch dead.'

To his exasperation, the girl began to weep. He should have remained his normal hectoring self, he reflected bitterly. In an attempt to retrieve the situation, he said harshly: 'Look, all the time you and I are here talking, you're paying for. If you want to pay for me to listen to you weep — well, it's your money. But when it's gone, I'll stop listening and throw you out.'

This verbal smack in the face dried up the tears with a jerk. Ros Kernwell regarded him with loathing.

'If I weren't honest, I'd be able to afford a better Tec than you!' she complained bitterly. 'A civil one, at any rate . . . '

'All right, all right! You're still wasting time.'

'Bizman Borrowitch employed me as his accountant because he preferred to keep his assets in visual art form rather than copyright. His account was with First Gold City Bank, so he already knew me, and he knew the Bank's opinion of me.'

'He didn't hire you because you were young and pretty?' interposed the Tec.

The girl half rose.

'Sit down,' drawled Denson. 'Remember you can't afford anyone else. I may have to ask you a lot worse questions than that before I'm through, so you'd better learn to keep your cool. I'll take the answer to that as 'no'. Here's another rude one: Are you really experienced, or might he have hired you because he thought you were a dope?'

'There are plenty of experts in the field

more experienced than I,' replied Ros tightly, 'but they would be more expensive, of course. Conversely, there are those who would be a lot cheaper, but know a lot less.'

'That doesn't entirely answer my question,' grunted the Tec.

'Only Borrowitch could have answered for his motives. Why don't you summon his shade and cross-examine *him?*' retorted the woman, the bitterness back in her voice.

'It might be easier than talking to you!' responded Denson. 'What happened that would give City Investigators reason to suspect you?'

'They've had the picture collection at the bank audited. Most of them are fakes.'

The Tec stared. 'How come you didn't realise that?'

'Because the last time I checked on them they were genuine. The switch must have taken place after that.'

'But City Investigators don't believe that? They think you disposed of the pictures some time ago?'

'Yes,' replied Ros.

'But then why would you kill Borrowitch? The last thing you would want to do, if you knew the pictures had been substituted, would be to draw attention to the collection by bumping off the owner.'

'Tec Garwen — the man from City who interrogated me — he suggests that I panicked and murdered him.'

'Poison isn't a panic weapon,' objected Sarn Denson.

'Garwen says people don't always act rationally — especially if they panic.'

'I take it you have an Accusation Policy?'

The woman nodded.

'Who is it with?'

'Aurum Life.'

The Tec sighed. 'You certainly do complicate things. Of course, if they were to accuse you, they couldn't also act for you — they'd have to lay off the policy with some other company. Still, they don't have to do anything until you are formally accused, and you can't claim under the policy until they do. My guess is that they'll stall on the formalities until they've got a cast iron case.'

The woman watched, silently.

'Where did the Bizman actually die?'

'At his house in Shatter Hill.'

'That's an expensive area — all single-column developments, aren't they?'

Ros nodded. 'The Borrowitch household has its own column in a hundred hectare park. There are ten pods attached when everyone's at home, but that doesn't happen very often.'

'Tell me about his family.'

'Adelin Borrowitch is — was — his second wife. She's a sculptress, but not much of her work is bankworthy. It might do as loose change at a drinkshop.'

'Younger than Borrowitch?' interrupted the Tec.

Ros nodded vigorously. 'Much younger. She's about the same age as Zarah, Edlin's daughter by his first marriage.'

'Zarah lives at the column?'

'Yes, some of the time. When she's there, she's with her boyfriend, Arick Earthborn. Sometimes they go off together, though.'

'Is that his real name?' questioned the Tec.

13

Ros shrugged. 'I don't know. He's an actor, if he can be said to actually *do* anything, so probably not.'

'Pity,' sighed Denson. 'Old Earth interests me. It would be fascinating to meet someone with a patryonic harking back to the Expansion. However, I can't imagine it's relevant to your difficulties. Who else hangs from the column?'

'The Bizman has two sons, also by his first marriage. They live there when they've insufficient lucre to live anywhere else.'

'Any attachments?'

'They don't bring them to the column if they have. Lastly, there's Nadya Lasolere. She's a friend of Adelin's.'

'Any of them have any motives for killing the Bizman?'

'Any one of them, I shouldn't wonder,' replied Ros.

'You don't like them?'

'None of them have ever given me any reason to,' said Ros shortly.

'Was it well known that Borrowitch had a large insurance policy?'

'Of course. There's no deterrent in a

large policy if you don't advertise it.'

Tec Denson nodded. 'So the killer had a very compelling motive, serious enough for him (or her) to risk the sort of intensive investigation that a large policy buys . . .'

He stood up. 'There will be other questions I want to ask you, but I don't know what they are yet. I'll have to dig around a bit, then I'll see you again. Oh, and I stipulate the usual one-man operator exclusion: if at any point it becomes apparent that one of the mobs is responsible, I'll drop out and make no charge. Tackling the gangs is a job for the big Tec agencies, not for one man bands.'

Ros Kernwell rose. 'Are you going to question the Borrowitch family?'

Denson shook his head. 'Not yet. They'd just refuse to talk to me, and there's no way in which I could compel them. I need something on them first, something that will make them speak to me rather than risk staying silent. It'll take me a little while to find what I need.'

'Supposing you don't find anything?'

'I will,' promised Sarn, although some

doubt assailed him, as it always did at the start of the case.

'There might be nothing to find,' persisted Ros.

'There's always something,' asserted Denson, 'especially when it's rich people you're dealing with. Everyone has something to hide, not necessarily anything criminal, but something which conflicts so seriously with their own image of themselves, that they will do almost anything to prevent anyone else discovering it . . . '

2

A Tec Investigates

After the girl had gone. Sarn Denson bathed, ate and then slept. He woke as Aurum sank in the south, leaving a golden glow in the evening sky. His depression had disappeared, and he felt hungry. He sat at his table and pushed the breakfast button. The top slid back and a meal rose from within the table. He had his cooker randomly programmed for breakfasts, so it was always a surprise, although he retained selective ordering for his other meals.

By the time he was ready to leave, night had come and the city welcomed it with a blaze of light. Denson's home column stood on the steep slopes to the landward side of the metropolis, and, looking down from an observation port, he could see the full extent of the urban zone. It glittered with multicoloured neon and laser lights. Lines of luminescence traced out the pattern of throughways and boulevards, streets and alleyways. Buildings blazed forth like beacons. The air was clear, and the light and the dark were sharply divided.

Denson left the view to look after itself, and went through his connecting module to the column branch. He walked down the passage towards the column where the lift shafts were. Just before he reached them, he stopped at a door in the side of the corridor.

He pressed his thumb on the lock, and the door swung outward. He passed through into his garage and the door closed behind him. The Tec got into his car. The outer doors of the garage opened, and the car slid out on to the cableway.

There was a stiff wind coming up from the valley, and the car swayed a little. Denson drove slowly until his cable intersected with the communal cable from the column, and then he accelerated. The wheels above him hummed as they raced along the metal hawser.

Soon the column cableway joined the main cable which ran down the valley. There was very little traffic and he was able to run on the wire without slackening speed. The view he had spurned now spread itself before him again. The gradient added impetus to the car's own propulsion, and he raced along, suspended high above the ground.

As Denson's car approached the city, lines turned off the main cableway and veered towards outlying sectors of the metropolis. The Tec kept on towards the city centre, but he slowed his speed as the wire was becoming crowded with cable cars. The main cable itself now divided and re-divided, and soon the cableway had half a dozen parallel strands carrying traffic in towards the urban heart. Snooper cars from the Gold City Cable Company slid by, alert for toll dodgers.

Above the cables flared advertisements for the massive insurance companies, and for the myriad lesser businesses and traders who catered for the diverse needs of the city's inhabitants. Interspersed with the commercial messages were route directions, but Denson hardly needed to watch the glowing signs that hung in the air a few metres above the cableway. He knew the turning he needed, and well beforehand he was slipping from the inner fast cable towards the outer, slower strands, in good time to take the northbound slipway which led towards the commercial sector of the city.

The cableway rapidly lost height as it threaded its way through the canyons of offices and commercial buildings. These were solid blocks of permanent offices, warehouses and factories, not like the columnar residential structures with their everchanging collections of modules. They were brightly lit, since the working life of the city pulsed through the night as strongly as it beat during the day. Other cars sped past him in both directions, their lights a brilliant flash, their wheels humming on the cables.

Occasionally a commercial vehicle ground past in the opposite direction, or he overtook one creaking along on the slow wire.

Denson slowed his car again and

changed wheel-sets on to a new cable that had begun. As soon as the second wheel-set was securely on the new cable, he withdrew the first from the original wire and thus transferred his car to the new direction. This took him north-east, through a dimmer part of the town, on a little frequented throughway leading towards the shore.

Before long, traffic picked up again and lights brightened until, when he emerged on to Shore Boulevard, it was as busy as the centre of the city. Traffic here was slower and less purposeful, however, as lovers and holidaymakers cruised in the starlight by the dark and heaving ocean.

The Tec's destination was a vast arcade at the northern end of the boulevard. He steered his car into the reception channel and parked it in an empty cable bay. He got out and took an escalator to the floor he sought.

Denson needed to consult the data banks. Like everything else in Gold City, these were run on a strictly commercial basis. Firms specialised in the type of information they accumulated — commercial, fiscal, social, criminal, gossip, rumour, history, international affairs, sport, science, technology, meteorology — there were hundreds of specialist companies, each gleaning, sorting and storing information. Fact or fiction, true or false, important or trivial, somebody in this vast building would store it. If a firm acquired information which it couldn't store, it would sell it to a company who could.

For a novice to uncover data in this huge emporium, it could be very expensive, but over the years, Denson had learned his way around the market, as did all successful Tecs. He went first to Biography (Dorado) Incorporated. Once there, a bored compop photocopied his credit card and waved him to a VDU booth. Denson sat down and activated the Visual Display Unit. He quickly wrote the name of Bizman Borrowitch on the screen with a Light Pencil. The name vanished instantaneously and text replaced it on the viewer:

Edlin Borrowitch. Bizman. Born 14-7-3072 Standard Date. Married 3101 SD,

Gloria Maklen by whom 3 children, daughter Zarah born 3102 SD, son Obert born 3104 SD, son Jaimi born 3105 SD. Widowed 3127 SD. Married Adelin Jowns 3129 SD. Address 53rd column, Shatter Hill Sector, Gold City.

Owner Borrowitch Textiles (Dorado) Incorporated. Estimated wealth 400,000 Leonardos. Business address Borrowitch Tower, Strand Sector, Gold City.

Bank First Gold City. Factories: South Sector, Gold City; Old Suburb, City of Golden Hill; Mount Three Sector, Straits Bridge City, Southern Continent. Associated companies: Textiles Marketing Incorporated of Startown; Fantasy Fabrics of Joy City (See separate entries under Thirlward MEERAN and Shani CHANDON). Interests . . .

Sarn Denson took a copy of the biography and tried Adelin Borrowitch, but the screen displayed a brief 'Try Gossip Associates'. He got the same response for Nadya Lasolere. He wasted no expenditure on the Bizman's children, sensing they'd have nothing the stolid

Biography Incorporated would feel was worth recording, but on impulse he tried Arick Earthborn, and was astonished at the length of the entry.

Arick Earthborn, alias Arick Snellskift (Earthborn was mother's patryonymic). Actor. Graduate of Dorado Academy of Drama. Studied Strafford on Altair 5. Leading roles in Merak 2 repertory. Returned Dorado 3130 SD. Prime mover in attempts to establish non-video theatre in Gold City. Played lead in 'Earthlight', 'Venus in Centauri' . . .

Tec Denson felt he had underestimated this Arick Earthborn. He was obviously a go-getter, no parasite it would seem.

The Tec left Biography Incorporated and descended to a lower level of the building, where Gossip Associates (Dorado) Inc. purveyed their data. Unlike the sober offices of Biography Incorporated, those of Gossip were plush and inviting. They were always well patronised, usually by people of a seedier kind than those who utilised the other stores in the building.

Men and women came here to spend their money prying into the lives and scandals of the rich and famous, important and notorious. Nothing that went into Gossip's files was checked for accuracy. The flimsiest rumour was grist to their mill. Consequently, anything he learned here, Sarn Denson knew, he must take with buckets of salt, but he might get a clue.

He keyed in Adelin Borrowitch. A single line came up on the screen.

INFORMATION BOUGHT OUT.

Now that's interesting, thought the Tec, far more significant than any gossip might have been. It wasn't cheap to buy information 'out' of Gossip's files. Too many blanks like that, and nobody would bother to come to them, so their price was high — blackmail, as some people described it. It seemed certain that only the Bizman could have afforded to censor whatever the file had contained — unless Adelin came from a rich family herself. Denson tried Nadya Lasolere and received the same message. That really made him think.

He pursed his lips and called up Zarah Borrowitch. This time he was rewarded with a lengthy report on the gossip surrounding her association with Arick Earthborn, much of it mildly salacious, all of it highly malicious. What interested Denson was that it was still here on file. If it was the Bizman who had bought out the data on his wife and her friend, whatever it contained must have been pretty unpleasant, since he hadn't bothered to clear out his daughter's entry.

Denson next tried Borrowitch's sons. On one he drew a blank, but the younger son, Jaimi, had considerable space allotted to him. It didn't amount to a great deal, most of it being in the style 'Prominent Bizman's son seen at Garillio's; Textile baron's offspring barred from Nordam's' and so on. All the named establishments were gambling halls, and Jaimi Borrowitch appeared to be a prodigious loser, and capricious payer. It was a line he should pursue, decided the Tec.

Tec Denson left the information arcade feeling hungry. He took his cable car south along the Sea Boulevard until he left the business district behind and entered a pleasure zone. Here there were people walking in the streets below the cableway. He parked his car in a pay garage and joined the pedestrians.

It was a good-humoured crowd, intent on pleasure but in no hurry to reach a destination. He threaded his way through groups and loners. It was a warm night and the cafés and restaurants had their tables and benches out in the streets. The aroma of foods from a dozen different planets mingled in and enriched the air. Dorado's solitary moon was now high in the sky, its two perpendicular rings giving it the appearance of an immense orange gyroscope precessing across the star-strewn sky.

Denson stopped in front of a small, brightly-lit restaurant which specialised in salads and fish from the Altairian system. Remembering Arick Earthborn, the Tec sat down at one of the tables. The waiter, when he came, was

27

unmistakably Altairian — short and dark, eyes half closed, even at night. The Tec ordered, and then sat back to watch the passers-by, and the night sky, sampling the smells of food, perfume and salt sea. He drank sharp Altarian spirit, but sparingly, as the night was barely half spent, and there were things that needed doing.

The obvious lines of enquiry were Jaimi's gambling, and the murky secret (or secrets) of Adelin Borrowitch and Nadya Lasolere. If Jaimi were deeply in debt, he might have been tempted to hasten the day of his inheritance. Even if he hadn't, the suggestion that he could be suspected for doing so might make him talkative.

Whether there was an advantage to be gained from knowing the gossip about Adelin and Nadya that had been hushed up, he couldn't say, but the very mystery of it intrigued him, and he was determined to concentrate on that angle. He hoped it wouldn't turn out to be something as prosaic and unremarkable as a lesbian relationship. Odd how people covered up these non-criminal deviations even after centuries of acceptance of them by Society.

His meal finished, Denson left the restaurant, retrieved his cable car, and, turning off Sea Boulevard, threaded his way through a maze of narrow streets wide enough for only a single wire in each direction.

He crossed the main east-west thoroughfare and was once again in the commercial quarter, albeit a seedier part than earlier. He brought his car to a halt on a street parking cable, and stepped on to the catwalk of a tall but shabby building whose grubby dilapidation even the moonlight could not disguise. He turned through a doorway and climbed a narrow stair. Reaching a landing, he knocked at the wooden door which bore the legend: EFFEL STERNBLOOM DOMESTIC AGENCY.

A squeaky voice penetrated the heavy panels: 'Who is it?'

'Sarn Denson, your favourite Tec,' replied Denson.

He waited while the door file compared

his voice print with that stored in its memory. The door swung silently inward and he went through.

The office was dimly lit, bare, cold and uninviting. Denson concealed his distaste. The only furnishing the room boasted was a desk and a chair, and a row of data stores. On the desk was an audio communicator, and behind the desk, concealing the chair entirely, sprawled a mountainous woman, old and ugly, with tiny, half-closed eyes, bulbous, runny nose, and slack, down-curving mouth set between huge, quivering jowls. Her body cascaded floorwards, draped in a voluminous, yet not entirely adequate, black dress. Wisps of grey hair framed a matt white face. Two bulging and beringed hands rested on the desk. The knuckles whitened as Effel Sternbloom attempted to heave herself from her chair in greeting, but she had subsided like a gigantic landslide long before the Tec managed to mutter, 'Please don't get up.'

Bizwoman Sternbloom's mouth made a heroic effort to turn its ends up, threatening her whole face with collapse.

The glistening lips parted and from the depths of the human mountain, a squeak escaped: 'Hello, bright boy! Nice to see yer again!'

Denson felt rather uncomfortable. Although he could lie without a quiver in the course of duty, he found it impossible to utter a dishonest social sentiment with any pretence at sincerity, and was quite unable to return her empty greeting.

'What brings yer here?' squeaked Effel.

'I hoped you might be able to help me out,' replied the Tec.

'Sure thing!' piped the Bizwoman. 'I owe yer a favour. I always will. Nothing I can ever do for you will even the score, so ask away.'

'I wanted information about some people I'm investigating,' the Tec went on. 'I've tried Gossip, but they've been bought out. I reckoned there was a possibility that one of your agency staff might have picked something up.'

'Be specific, dearie!' fluted Sternbloom. 'I'm no hypotheticaliser — I can't theoreticise. Just give me the names.'

'I'm interested in two people,' replied

Denson, almost reluctantly, as though, whatever the stakes, no one deserved to have their names uttered in this sordid atmosphere. 'Their present labels are Adelin Borrowitch and Nadya Lasolere.'

Effel pursed her lips in a silent whistle, a singularly repulsive sight from which the Tec almost recoiled physically.

'You are moving in exalted circles, ain't yer?' trilled the quivering mass.

'Of course, I realise memories cost,' said Denson.

'Not from me!' protested Effel. 'I 'aven't forgotten what yer did for me. I'm obligated to yer for life, I am.'

'Still,' she considered, 'I'll need to jog some people. I'd gladly fork out meself, but staffing ain't what it used to be. So if yer could put up the stake for the greedy gubbins I'll have to squeeze, I'll do what I can for yer.'

'I knew you would,' responded the Tec, trying to put some enthusiasm into his voice. He fished a wad of Leonardos out of his wallet and pushed them across the desk. A huge paw scooped them up. Denson hastily averted his eyes from their ultimate destination.

'Oke,' he grunted. 'I'll be back tomorrow then.'

'Welcome you'll be, dearie,' grinned Effel Sternbloom. 'Course I can't guarantee anything by then, or ever, but I'll do my best for yer.'

'Thanks,' muttered Denson, and beat a hasty retreat.

3

Startown

Denson rose late on the following morning, like almost everyone else in Gold City. Gold City was not a morning town. The Tec stared from his window across the somnolent city to the unknown ocean beyond. After centuries of settlement, the continents of Dorado were no longer a mystery, but the wide, deep seas kept their secrets yet. No one knew what might lurk in the dark depths of their unbounded expanse, nor what surprises the thousands of islands might give the first human to invade their ancient solitude.

The Tec shivered. He was a creature of the city and thoughts of the wilderness disturbed him. He bent his mind to business, to the comforting routine of human depravity — for all its unpleasantness, human wickedness was nonetheless human.

He still had insufficient ammunition

with which to attack the Borrowitch family. He must wait on whatever Effel Sternbloom could dig up for him on the women, and it was no use following up Jaimi's passion for gambling until the establishments were open for business in the evening. He had, as yet, nothing on Obert, Zarah or Arick Earthborn, and he wasn't sure where to begin to crack them. For want of any better ideas, he decided to have a look at Edlin Borrowitch's business associates. They'd have no reason to clam up — probably would be glad to help uncover Borrowitch's assassin. Like all other professions, the Bizmen of Dorado stood together when one of their ilk was threatened or injured.

According to the Biography Incorporated file on Edlin Borrowitch, his closest business associates were Thirlward Meeran and Shani Chandon. Denson had consulted their biographies. Bizman Meeran was Chief Executive of Textiles Marketing Incorporated, which had its headquarters in Startown, where it was well placed for the extensive export trade with neighbouring systems. Bizwoman Chandon's Fantasy

Fabrics offices were in Joy City. A visit to Joy City would be more fun than one to Startown, but the latter was quite close and he could easily accomplish the return trip before evening.

Denson drove his car round to the outer ring cable and picked up the northbound cableway as it emerged from the city's suburbs. It was a ten strand highway and he made good time across the dense forest which separated the two major settlements on Dorado. He had driven for an hour or so when the wires began to rise higher above the treetops in preparation for the long swoop across Golden Creek. The car clicked past a pylon, and Sarn could see the arm of the ocean that was Golden Creek. It penetrated deep into the hinterland and the overland distance between Gold City and Startown had been cut dramatically when the cableway had first bridged it.

Denson's car rose to one final pylon, and then he was over the shining sea. Below him, the waves shattered the sunshine into sparkles that dazzled the eyes. To his left, the inlet wound away between wooded shores. To his right, it opened out into the unknown ocean. The inter-pylon distances across the loch were long and the cable sagged closer to the spume than the Tec liked. A rock jutting above the fjord's surface near the midpoint of the channel provided a foothold for a central pylon, without which the entire crossing would not have been feasible.

As usual, Denson felt relief flood through him as the cable crossed the northern shoreline. It felt warmer above the forest than it did above the water, but perhaps that was just his imagination.

It was mid-day when Denson penetrated the outskirts of Startown. To the east of the city was a spaceport, perched on the cliff-tops. A seemingly endless procession of shuttles rose seawards from the space terminal to rendezvous with the huge ships wallowing in orbit high above the planet's surface. Denson ignored them and concentrated on the cableplan of Startown which glowed on his mapscreen. The offices and warehouses of Textiles Marketing Incorporated were in the eastern environs of the city, close to the starport. He threaded his way through the tangled web of cables which opened out to reach the various quarters of the urbanopolis, rising above and dipping below cross cables, slipping aside at junctions, until he was in the spaceport approach.

He spied the offices of Textiles Marketing and took the cable that led right into their building, a solid box-like edifice like the commercial buildings of Gold City Centre rather than the columnar residential structures of that city's western hills.

As he stepped from his car, Denson was accosted by a smooth looking individual, who purred a greeting:

'Good day to you sir. What is your concern with us, may I ask?'

'I want to see Bizman Meeran on a personal matter,' replied the Tec irritably. Smoothies always irritated him. He knew it was unprofessional, even arrogant, but he couldn't help it.

'Personal for him or for you?' enquired the smoothie, with a hint of derision in his voice.

'Tell him I've come about Bizman Borrowitch,' growled Sarn, and handed the man a slip of plastic on which his name and title glowed.

'Ah, a sad event,' mourned the receptionist. 'I will see if Bizman Meeran is available.'

The receptionist stood motionless for a moment. Denson thought he could detect a slight movement of his throat as he communicated sub-vocally with someone, and guessed he must have a larynx mike and an ear receiver fitted.

'I am afraid that the Bizman himself is in conference,' the receptionist said, 'but his personal accountant, Abam Cluth, can see you.'

Denson was about to make a scene when he reflected that an interview with an Accountant might be useful. He could always insist on seeing the Bizman later.

'Please follow the guide,' directed the smoothie and took a small sphere from his pocket. He held it in the air, level with Sarn's eyes, and released it. It immediately began to move away slowly.

The Tec followed, and the sphere

speeded up, adjusting its pace to Denson's own. He followed it up some stairs and along a corridor, around a corner into plusher surroundings. The sphere stopped in front of a door and bleeped. After a moment the door swung open, and the sphere preceded Denson into the room. From the floating globe issued the voice of the receptionist:

'Tec Denson, Accountant A. Cluth.'

Sarn covertly sized up the man who sat behind the big empty desk. His skin was totally white, his lips bloodless. Only the black eyes gave colour to his face, which was framed with shoulder-length black hair of unnatural straightness. The Accountant was dressed in a black overall from the sleeves of which his white hands grew, the fingers taking root on the smooth surface of the desk. Without moving his hands at all, Cluth rose, and he was tall. His mouth opened in a smile of synthetic welcome and he inclined his head slightly.

'Well met, Tec Denson,' he greeted with precise diction, as colourless as his visage. 'We were all distressed to hear of the death of Bizman Borrowitch. We admired him for all his acumen. Bizman Meeran was especially saddened, as he was a friend as well as an associate of the deceased.'

'You were not a friend?' asked Denson bluntly.

'Don't be naïve, Tec Denson,' replied Cluth, his voice still expressionless. 'I'm an Accountant, not a Bizman. I respected Bizman Borrowitch, and I believe he valued my contribution to Textiles Marketing Incorporated, but we had no social relationship.'

'Then I don't see how you can help me,' said Denson flatly.

'You are investigating Borrowitch's death on behalf of Aurum Life?' There was an interrogative inflection in Cluth's voice, which Denson ignored.

'You knew Aurum Life was the Bizman's insurer?' Denson countered evasively.

'Of course,' replied Cluth. 'Nobody would conceal their life insurance arrangements — indeed I fancy there are those who pretend they have policies in order to frighten off would-be assassins.'

41

'I still don't see how you can help,' persisted the Tec. 'It's Meeran I really wanted to see.'

'What is it you want to know?' asked the Accountant.

'How Borrowitch seemed in himself — was he depressed, afraid, apprehensive? The sort of thing you'd notice in a social relationship, but which is normally concealed in a business one.'

'It is true we were not social equals,' conceded Cluth, 'but we spent a lot of time together on business matters. The Bizman was keen on expanding the export trade in textiles from Dorado, particularly to the Capella, Arcturus and Fomalhaut systems. Trans-stellar trade requires a substantial capital investment because of transport costs, and Bizman Borrowitch was very interested in the financial problems.'

'I don't think any of that is going to help me find out who killed Borrowitch,' grumbled Denson.

'I was just explaining that we did in fact see a lot of each other — we had a close business rapport,' insisted the Accountant. 'So I would have noticed if he had seemed depressed or frightened. He was worried sometimes, but we were dealing in large sums, and that was only to be expected.'

'The point is,' said Denson, 'that if he was worried about his family or apprehensive about something in his personal life, he would never have considered confiding in you. That's why I must talk to Bizman Meeran. He can't be so very busy, since he's wasting his time listening to you and I talk round in circles.'

There was an uncomfortable silence, and then a door opened, and a tall, bronzed man with a shock of white hair, strode into the room. He held out a hand to Denson, and a cheerful smile lit his face.

'I guess you're right, Tec Denson!' he agreed. 'It would be more profitable for us to get together — and profit's a good thing, eh?'

Denson took the Bizman's hand.

'Come into my office,' invited Meeran. 'You'll find it more comfortable than this counting house.'

He gave Cluth a cheery wave as he said

this, but Sarn noticed a certain sourness in the Accountant's expression.

'How did you know I was listening?' enquired the Bizman when they were seated in his sanctum.

'It was a guess,' admitted the Tec, 'based on the way Cluth was behaving. He gave me the impression he was being watched — or listened to, at any rate. He spoke as though he were dictating all the time, and he had that uneasy air of being on trial.'

The Bizman laughed. 'He's not the most relaxed man ever!'

He became more serious, and leaned towards Denson. 'You want to know if I noticed anything about Borrowitch's manner lately, or if he said anything to me about his personal problems.'

The Tec nodded.

Meeran leaned back again, and stared at the ceiling, a swirling orange mist like the atmosphere of some far — flung planet. Idly, Denson wondered how it was kept in place. The Bizman read his thoughts.

'It's a cold plasma,' he explained,

'magnetically constrained. I find it more restful to look at than a rigid surface.'

'I'll speak my mind to you,' he went on, 'since Borrowitch's death angers me. He was a fine man and a competent Bizman. I've lost a first class associate and a close acquaintance — not a friend exactly, but someone I was used to.'

He paused for a moment, in thought, then resumed: 'He said nothing to me about his personal life, nor anything about any fears he might have had either for himself or for the company. But he did seem unusually preoccupied about something. His manner towards me cooled noticeably. He seemed almost to try and avoid me. When we met, he was always anxious to conclude our business and then be on his way. I tried not to take offence. I told myself he was absorbed in the planning of our next big push into the Capella market. If he was nervy about it, who could blame him? I feel a trifle apprehensive myself.'

'Was it true that he spent a lot of time with your Accountant?'

The Bizman frowned. 'I suppose so.'

'More than with yourself?'

'Yes. Recently, anyhow. Borrowitch and I finished planning the merchandising side of the Capella operation some time ago. All that remained to be settled was the financing. I generally leave money matters very much in Cluth's hands.'

'Didn't it strike you as odd that Borrowitch didn't do the same? That is, leave his side of the arrangements to his own Accountant?'

'Ros Kernwell, you mean? I don't know. Borrowitch was definitely interested in the financial side of the business. It was his grasp of the economic facts of life that enabled him to accumulate so large a fortune from such small beginnings. I don't have his flair for money, that's why I rely on Cluth so heavily.'

Denson rose. 'Thank you for your help, Bizman Meeran.'

'Have I been of any help?' smiled the Bizman quizzically.

'At least you haven't hindered me — I hope!' grinned the Tec in return. 'It's too early in the case to know what will be useful and what won't.'

'You've no suspect as yet?' enquired Meeran.

'Not yet,' replied Denson.

They walked together towards the door.

'Aurum Life has a reputation for success,' ventured the Bizman. 'I'm sure you won't fail in the present instance.'

'I agree with your assessment of Aurum Life's reputation,' replied Denson innocently, 'but that has no bearing on whether I succeed or fail, since I am not employed by them. Good business!'

The Tec left the Bizman staring after him, a frown of annoyance on the big man's face.

★ ★ ★

Denson was preoccupied on the return journey. Textiles Marketing seemed to him a curiously run outfit, and neither Cluth nor Meeran had struck him as straightforward individuals. He began to think he might have been over-hasty in suspecting that a member of Borrowitch's household was the murderer. The Bizman's business associates might bear closer investigation.

Pondering these thoughts, he paid no heed to the garish structures he passed, the head offices of interstellar trading giants like Arcturus Combine, Spica Trading, Aldebaran Merchants Incorporated and Fomalhaut Import-Export. Many interplanetary companies had their headquarters on Dorado, the only civilised world to have no government to regulate their affairs.

The Tec's car had left the city far behind and was riding high above the forest. The mid-day traffic was light. Ahead of him, the pylons were taller still as the cableway approached Golden Creek. Soon he was soaring up and out over that arm of the sea. He peered down at the mysterious looking water. It was said that, even on Old Earth, not all the creatures that lurked in that planet's deepest oceans had been documented by marine biologists, despite more than a millenium of exploration and study. How much less must the investigation of Aurum's seas be? There were stories of strange monsters which terrorised the credulous, and Denson was not immune to them.

He would be glad to be back in the city, where the dangers came in human guise.

He had passed the central pylon, perched on its rocky islet, and was heading fast for the southern shoreline when disaster struck. The car gave a sickening lurch, and the wheels whirred above him. The car listed badly, and fear clutched at Sarn's stomach. He fought to control the vehicle, knowing all the time that it was beyond his power to do so.

Abruptly the car and its over-carriage parted, and he plummeted towards the heaving surface of the hostile sea . . .

4

Panic

When Ros Kernwell left Tec Sarn Denson's office, she was feeling more cheerful. Some of the weight of suspicion that had weighed on her, she felt, was in some way transferred to the Tec. As she steered her car slowly along the winding cableway that led through the foothills to the west of the city, she even found the courage to take pleasure in the deep blue of the sky and the brown and gold of the rocks that stood silhouetted against it.

The canyon floor was barren, scoured bare by the periodic floods which swept through it when storms deluged the uplands. Here and there, huge nuggets of gold glinted in the rich rays from Dorado's sun, and Ros fell to musing on the metal which was so common on Dorado, and yet so rare on all other settled planets that, until the discovery of

Dorado, it had served as the basis for local currencies and interstellar exchange alike.

Gold was indeed so plentiful on Dorado that even the city streets were paved with it — alloyed with other metals to make it last longer. There was a city on Old Earth — maybe only a mythical city — whose streets were said to be paved with gold. But the innocents who believed that were disappointed when drawn by the saying they flocked to its streets — the gold was only metaphorical. Nobody would come to Dorado because of its golden pavements. The whole planet was loaded with gold so that it was the cheapest metal available. In the initial euphoria, Gamma Doradus II became known throughout the civilised worlds as Dorado, and its sun, Gamma Doradus, was renamed Aurum after the ancient derivation of the chemical symbol for gold. The discovery of Dorado had undermined the entire interstellar economy and destroyed Earth's hegemony, based as it was on the prehistoric gold standard.

Once gold became so common as to be

worthless, some other medium of value had to be found. Not that gold had ever been freighted about the Universe to pay for things — that would have been a shocking waste of payload. Being the oldest inhabited planet, and the most extensively exploited, Earth had had the largest stocks of gold. They remained on the old planet physically, but credits were transferred electronically from world to world. So Earth Bank was the financial centre of the interstellar trading community, and gave the home planet tremendous power over the early colonists, a power which Dorado had shattered simply by being discovered.

When the fiscal system collapsed, another medium of exchange was sought, and it was an Earth banker who came up with the answer. In accepting his suggestion, the interstellar community accepted the pre-eminence of Earth in trade once more, but this time the medium of exchange was itself of real value, sufficient to be worth accepting for star freight, and thus in principle it was at least possible that the centre of commercial power could be removed from Earth. Certainly right from the beginning it brought about a gradual diminution of Earth's economic overlordship.

The medium chosen was art! It sounded simple and obvious now that people had grown used to it, but at first it was so revolutionary as to be incomprehensible. Now that the system had shaken down, it functioned very smoothly. An interplanetary consortium of bankers, artists and others valued works of art in terms of a basic credit unit of artistic value.

The base of the system was a painting by Vargon, which was reckoned to be just about worth the cost of shipping from Earth to Alpha Centauri under the ancient commercial regime. Anything of lesser value was relegated to local planetary currency. Anything more was valued in terms of how many Vargons someone would be willing to swap for it.

If experts were in doubt, it would be auctioned to discover exactly that. Of course the value of any given work of art — painting, sculpture, carving or whatever — was always the highest bid. Values changed too, but then they always had done with the old metal-based currencies.

A beneficial side-effect was that colonial systems began to receive works of art from the Old Planet, part of the cultural heritage of the whole race which had hitherto been mouldering in Earth's museums, export very largely forbidden. It also encouraged local art, not only stimulating people to attempt artistic creation, but also develop canons of taste based on the comparison of art in terms of Vargons. It sounded crude, but in fact it led to a great deal of serious thought about artistic value in general, and individual works of art in particular.

Literature and music were included in the cultural reserve system by extension of the old copyright laws, valued of course in Vargons. Those ancient antithetical institutions, banks and museums, once the outward symbols of commercialism on the one hand and culture on the other, merged. The local bank and the local museum became one and the same, the assets of one being the exhibits of the other.

It was easy to understand how all law and order had collapsed in those early days of settlement on Dorado, where everyone thought they would be rich because the planet seemed to be made of gold. Miners and prospectors couldn't be expected to understand that the glut would render the precious metal valueless. Hadn't gold been prized by men since before the dawn of history? Wasn't it a metal of real beauty? What they had failed to appreciate was that its economic valuation had increased to an extent far beyond that intrinsic worth.

To begin with, no one foresaw the collapse. Everyone on Dorado was busy collecting gold. No policeman or government official sent to Dorado would then remain a law officer or civil servant. There was more gold to be picked up in one day than he could earn in a lifetime on a government salary. So law and order, government and public services had all collapsed on the golden planet. Then the whole interstellar economy had disintegrated, and, by the time it began to recover, Dorado had evolved its own peculiar and entirely commercial social system.

Ros wondered how it would feel to live on one of those other worlds, where governments provided law agencies to investigate crimes and to protect people. She was well versed in the arguments against them — the peril of tyranny, the infringement of liberty, the risk of corruption, the fear that a monopoly in the field of crime investigation would lead to all those other abuses to which other monopolies led — inefficiency, intransigence, aloofness, disregard of public interest and self-perpetuating aggrandizement.

Yet, in her extremity of need, Accountant Kernwell might have welcomed a guardian of law and order such as existed on Spica II or Alpha Proxima I, or the attentions of the 'Space Squad' that policed the Præsepe cluster. Here on Dorado, she could expect no independent investigation of the facts. Should she be formally charged before a Computer Court for the murder of the Bizman, then her own insurance policy would be activated . . . but would it be too late?

Irrationally, perhaps, Ros feared it would, hence her hiring of the Tec. She had not been overly impressed by him, but at least she no longer felt alone, and this feeling stayed with her until she emerged from the canyon and entered the dormitory suburb of Bandrye. It remained with her until she she had reached her own column, stowed her cable car in her garage, and walked the short distance out from the central stem to her own module. Then it left her, for there lounging against her door was the feared and detested figure of Tec Garwen.

Tec Garwen had been waiting a long time, and the delay had had a disagreeable effect upon his temper. He was already somewhat soured by an interview with his immediate superior at City Investigators Incorporated, Senior Tec Benit, who had castigated him for lack of progress. It was obvious, according to Benit, who the murderer was, so why was there as yet insufficient evidence to lay a charge? Garwen had protested about the difficulty of getting evidence in cases such as this.

Then what about a confession? Come on, Garwen, toughen up, had been Benit's valediction.

When Garwen had arrived at Ros Kernwell's module, he was feeling somewhat unhappy at having to brow-beat the girl. She was, after all, a personable young woman, and Garwen was a susceptible and basically soft-hearted man — where personable young women were concerned, at any rate. However, the enforced inactivity in the cramped passage leading to the suspect's module had hardened his cardiac organ and dimmed his memory of the Accountant's physical attraction. He transferred his grievance from Benit to the girl and, by the time she showed up, he was practically fuming.

'Where've you been?' he growled.

Ros's heart had sunk when she saw the bane of her existence hovering at her door, but she was not lacking in spirit. 'Go and find out!'

'Oh no, I want to talk to you . . . ' replied Garwen.

'Well *I* don't want to talk to *you* any more!' countered Ros firmly. 'Go away!'

'You can talk to me, or answer to a Justice Company Computer!' said Garwen harshly.

'Have you filed a charge?' asked Ros.

'Not yet, but we will if you don't co-operate.'

Ros Kernwell thought for a minute. If she were formally arraigned, then her insurance policy would become operative and she would at least have funds to prepare a defence. On the other hand, once a charge had been filed, there was a certain inevitability about the train of events. There was an agreed time limit for the preparation of the defence, unless a case could be made for an adjournment. Ros was reluctant to face the finality of a committal. Besides, she told herself, she had just engaged a Tec to accumulate evidence in her defence. Despite his roughness and apparently mercenary outlook, Denson had taken the case on. Surely she ought to try and gain some time in which he would have a chance to deliver the goods. Thus she persuaded herself that her reluctance to face immedi-ate arraignment was really common sense

59

rather than fear, and allowed herself to be subjected to further interrogation.

'You'd better come inside,' she acceded wearily.

When they were seated within the module, a small four roomed apartment, Tec Garwen began to go over her statements yet again. This time, however, he pressed hard on salient points, allowed his disbelief at denials of complicity to show, was openly derisive of her assertions of innocence. Skilfully, he built the tension, careful to avoid driving her to tears or hysteria before the climax of his interrogation was reached.

Under his remorseless scourging, Ros was beginning to crumble, beginning to feel it would be better to admit guilt rather than suffer this nerve-shredding questioning a moment longer. Garwen sensed her failure of nerve and prepared to administer the final blow, when his attention was distracted by a voice in his ear.

The Tec cursed the office transmitter which had directed the signal to his tiny receiver, but he was forced to listen to the sarcasm of his superior: 'Something has just come in which might be of use to you, and as you seem to be floundering about, I thought you'd better have it straight away.'

He spoke rapidly, and, by the time he'd finished, Garwen had ceased swearing under his breath. When the transmission was complete, the Tec turned his attention once more to Ros. She had guessed the reason for his sudden preoccupation and had taken the opportunity to compose herself. Garwen resumed his interrogation, seeking to regain the ground the interruption had lost him. Abruptly, he changed tack.

'You hired a Tec!' he accused.

Ros was startled, but in retrospect not surprised that he should have learnt that so soon. It was obviously the subject of his call.

'Yes I have,' she admitted. 'Wouldn't you?'

Garwen ignored this sally.

'Did you pay him in advance?' he asked.

'What business is that of yours?'

'I'm interested,' returned Garwen equably. 'You see, he's disappeared.'

'You're lying!' blurted out Ros.

Feigning a weary sadness, Garwen shook his head. 'Try contacting him,' he invited.

'I don't need to,' countered Ros firmly. 'I know you're lying. You're trying to frighten me, or trap me, or something.'

Garwen rose. 'Have it your own way,' he said, 'but reality will catch up with your illusions before long.'

He crossed to the door and let himself out, without even glancing back. When he had gone, Ros Kernwell sat still for minutes on end, her fists clenched in her lap, her knuckles white beneath her already pale skin. Abruptly, she went to her communicator and put out a call for Tec Denson. There was no response.

Fiercely, she fought down the panic that rose inside her. Until this moment, she hadn't realised just how much hope she had pinned on Denson. Now he had deserted her, and she felt defenceless. She lost the fight against panic; she forgot that were she formally accused, her insurance would then pay for an investigation. Her response to the situation was irrational and perhaps foolish, but her wits had deserted her. She could see only one way of escape from her predicament — flight.

When this solution presented itself, her panic came under control. She began to think clearly and methodically once more. Yet there was no reconsidering her decision to flee. It was as if that decision represented a discontinuity in her rational thought. The mental processes leading to that decision were beyond the reach of her new lucidity. Calmly now, she sat and thought out a plan of escape.

Ros Kernwell took time to select those of her possessions which combined value with compactness. To them she added the best of a representative collection of her clothing, and a few objects and papers that in some way contributed to her sense of identity — the first valuable fluorospar carving she had discovered in a junk shop, a small notebook in which she had jotted attempts at poetry, a cube that projected pictures of her parents and her childhood, a list of all her ancestors going back five generations.

She loaded these treasures into her cable car, and whirled down into the urbanopolis. She withdrew her savings from the bank, regretfully relinquishing her title to a Canaletto that was held in the vault. She bought some high-energy content provisions and crammed them into the remaining space in her vehicle, and finally set off again, heading south.

Before reaching the city limits, however, she slipped into the slow lane and left the main cableway, cutting across the city in a series of jagged sweeps along busy boulevards, until she joined the westbound cableway. She worked her car rapidly across the humming hawsers until she was in the fast lane, and so headed out on the intercity route towards Joy City.

Ros Kernwell did not as yet know what she would do when she reached her destination. Her idea was to lie low until the policy on the Bizman's life was exhausted — as soon as the money ran out, Aurum Life would lose interest and call off City Investigators. The trouble was, Borrowitch's life insurance was sure to have been very substantial. It seemed certain that she would run out of funds long before her pursuers.

Well, she told herself grimly, that was one very good reason for making for Joy City. She remembered Obert once saying that Joy City was the only place on Dorado where it was possible to make money in ways that didn't involve paper qualifications and recommendations, especially if you were a young and attractive woman. Ros didn't like the possibility of what she might be driven to, but penal servitude she relished even less. The prospect of being sold to one of the prison companies for a term of forced labour long enough to compensate for the Bizman's murder made her shake with fear . . .

5

Lucky Strike

Denson knew his car would sink as soon as it hit the water. As it fell seaward, he wrenched open the door and then waited for what seemed like an age, but it could not have been more than a few seconds, since the vehicle had begun its plunge. He held tight until the car hit the water, so that its body and not his own would take the shock of the impact, and then leaped clear.

The water was thick with algae at this time of the year, and he felt as if he was swimming in soup. As the cold of the water closed around him, he had gasped involuntarily and taken a mouthful of the nauseating brew. He spouted it out, and suppressed with some difficulty the urge to vomit.

He struck out shorewards, and, as he lifted his arms from the water, they trailed long filaments of yellow. There was a deep rolling swell in the inlet. In the troughs, he was isolated, surrounded by watery walls which rose skyward. On the crests, he could see the distant coastline, but in neither case was there any cause for hope.

However, Denson was not a man to give up. He plugged on, smothering despair and the fear of the unknown horrors which might lurk below the burgeoning weed, by concentrating his thoughts on the accident, and its probable cause. He felt it was most unlikely that it had been a real accident. Such failures rarely occurred. It was more likely that someone had deliberately sabotaged his machine. A bolt partially severed would have remained unbroken, but increasingly weakened by the motion of the car until it eventually gave under the strain. How long that would take would depend upon the depth of the cut. He had had the car serviced a month ago, so it must have occurred since then. Most probably, it was of a much more recent date — a would-be assassin would wish to reduce to a minimum the time during which the tampering might be discovered.

Did the shore seem closer? He decided to believe that it did — anything that would bolster his failing strength should be accepted with gratitude. He doubted that he could simply float through the clinging morass if he should become too tired to swim.

Wearily he crawled to the crest of another roller, and unbelievably saw the cruiser.

It was flying low over the water directly beneath the high cable. It zigzagged tightly as if searching for something — could it be looking for him? He summoned up a final effort and raised an arm above the algae, as he began to slide down the slope of the wave. The gesture threw him off balance and his head dipped below the surface of the soup. He felt the slimy tendrils over his face and in his ears. He kept his mouth firmly closed and his nostrils constricted, his eyes shut tight against the vile brew.

He seemed to go down for a very long time before he rose again, his lungs bursting, his feet treading water with the weary motion of an exhausted athlete. Desperately he cast about with his eyes, and there was the cruiser, and it was making directly for him. Hope released a last reserve of energy, and he trod water determinedly as the craft drew nearer. A line snaked down and he grabbed it gratefully.

The cruiser hovered ever nearer. A ladder followed the rope, and he transferred his grip, but he had not the strength to haul himself out. A bay opened in the belly of the cruiser and a boat was dropped.

A man scrambled down another ladder into the boat, and steered across to Denson. Gratefully, the Tec relinquished the ladder and flung his arms over the side of the dinghy. Carefully, the man hauled him aboard, and Sarn briefly registered the man's protective clothing and synthetic gauntlets and mask.

The cruiser was now hovering directly overhead. Hawsers rode gently down, and the man attached them to the boat, which was then drawn smoothly up into the interior of the flier.

Denson soon recovered from his ordeal. He learned that the carrier of his car had not come off the cable but had run back down towards the northern shore, until it struck a following car. The driver had radioed his insurance company and they had been able to identify Denson's own insurers from the number clearly visible on the carrier, whereupon Denson's own insurance company had dispatched a cruiser to search for him. He had been very lucky.

'You recovered the carrier?' Denson asked.

'You'll have to ask head office about that,' replied the patrol leader. 'We only came to look for you.'

Denson had a quick check-over by the company's doctor, plus a series of anti-allergy injections in case of reaction against Dorado's alien biota.

He went home, where he cleaned up and felt better. He filed his claim with his insurers and asked about the carrier. It had been recovered, but the bolts which should have held the car were missing. They must have dropped off when the car came loose. There was no evidence to show whether it was sabotage or an accident, and the insurance company were not interested.

Although the Tec carried a heavy life policy as a deterrent (he hoped) against assassination, he couldn't afford an attempted murder policy. Furthermore, it would hardly inspire confidence in prospective clients if it were known that he didn't trust himself to be able to investigate attempts at his own life. But the overriding factor was the prohibitive cost. Being a Tec was a high risk occupation. The premiums on his life policy were high enough, and that could only be claimed against once, if he was unlucky. An attempted murder policy might be invoked many times, and the companies were understandably wary about underwriting them.

He glanced at the digital wall clock and realised that the day was practically spent. He pressed a button in the arm of his chair, and the blinds of the room rolled up. In the south, the sun was setting in a blaze of gold. The sky was a deep yellow, and high flat clouds streaked bands of red and orange across it. In the north, the heavens were already darkening and the more luminous stars burned brilliant dots upon it.

He sat watching and waiting until the sun had sunk, so that he could just make out the faint starlight of the feeble Sol, the distant sun of that Earth which was never far from the thoughts of her children scattered through her wide skies. One day, when he pulled a really lucrative case, Denson dreamed he would turn his detective talents to genealogy. He would trace his line back through the records of Aurum Population Registration Incorporated, and whatever other systems to which the trail might take him, until he reached Old Earth.

He wondered if Sol was still a solitary star when his ancestors had left, or if Jupiter had already been ignited to make the Sol system a weak binary. Perhaps some of them had even dwelt on one of the Jovian satellites, given life by the kindling of the giant planet.

With a sigh, the Tec roused himself. He

changed into a smarter jump-suit, and took his new cable car down into the city. His route took him through the banking quarter, past the imposing head offices of First Gold City Bank, the flamboyant arcade which housed the Golden Sculpture Bank, the austere monolith of Earth Picture Bank, the sober edifice of Interstellar Copyright Bank, and the quiet pile of its rival, the Transworld Literature Bank. The ultramodern headquarters of the recently founded Aurum Artists Bank was in hideous contrast with the rococo style of the Spheres Music Bank. In incongruous juxtaposition to these commercial and cultural institutions, loomed the stark fortress of Mercenaries Incorporated, the nearest equivalent to an army which Dorado possessed.

Abruptly the cableway left the stolid world of business, and ran into the wire boulevard of the Lucky Strike. A dozen wires ran up and down the famous centre of Gold City gambling.

Lights blazed and lasers flared across the sky above the cables. On either side of the street garishly lit buildings advertised the opportunity to make a quick fortune. 'Win the Mona Lisa!' one establishment proudly boasted. 'Take home Marmot's Vision of Vega!' shrieked another — literally shrieked, for it wasn't only with lights that the gambling emporiums advertised. Electronic barkers withered the ear as the neon blinded the eye. Exotic perfumes wafted across the boulevard to entice pedestrians to follow their noses to the chance of a lifetime.

Denson parked the car and descended to the street. Holiday crowds thronged the wide expanse, laughing and talking, strolling and jostling. But here and there, Denson's practised eye picked out the more sombre visage; the furtive puposefulness of the inveterate gambler, the man or woman not out for a holiday flutter, but drawn by irresistable compulsion to the tables, to the race machines, to the radioactivity counters, to the random number generators, or to any of the multitude of forms which gambling took in the artistic avenue of the city's Lucky Strike Boulevard.

The Tec walked through the multi-coloured portal of the nearest gambling palace. He ignored the camera which he knew would be trained upon him, comparing his face with the rogues gallery stored in its memory, the many faces that were not welcomed by the management. The garish entrance led to a dimly lit passage, at the far end of which was a dazzling opening. He passed along the corridor, and through the inner doorway, into the brilliance beyond.

The brightness and the din were excessive. Strobes dappled the distant walls and the vaulted ceiling. Red, yellow, green, blue, orange and purple spotlights sped across the floor. The gamblers themselves for the most part dressed in sympathy with their surroundings. Jump suits and gowns twinkled and flashed with jewels and metal filigree. Faces powdered with gold shone in the speeding lights, nails gleamed and fluo-resced.

From high in the dome of the gambling

hall, music pealed and then cascaded upon the unheeding throng. Above the melodies, shrill voices trilled, while deeper tones bored through the endless pressure of sound. Like dark stains on a cloth of gold, the real gamblers moved. Unlike the brilliant dilettantes, they did not stroll from machine to machine, losing a little here, a little there, laughing and talking, hailing friends and rivals; they, for the most part, haunted but one favourite machine, which they beseiged with the passion of a besotted lover. Feverishly, they played their luck against the odds. They spoke to no one, they had no friends but the machine, they had no rival but the machine.

Was Jaimi Borrowitch one such? He hoped not. It would be useless to approach the management for information — they would say nothing about a client, or a former client, whatever they thought of him. He must hope to find someone here amongst the gamblers who was a friend of Jaimi's and not averse to gossiping.

Denson drifted from machine to

machine, trying his luck here and there, mentally chalking his losses up to the expenses he never really expected to collect. He listened to the chatter around him, getting himself in the mood of the place. Occasionally people would stand idly watching him, the way people do in gambling euphoria. When that happened, he seized the opportunity to engage them in conversation by exclaiming at his bad luck, or ruefully inviting them to try theirs. He would then mention his friend Jaimi Borrowitch, and watch for a flicker of recognition, but he drew a blank. Once he caught a glimpse of a face he thought he knew, but the man was swallowed up in the crowd, and Denson was left with an elusive memory.

The Tec moved on to the other gambling houses, losing money steadily, and gaining no information at all until he reached the Golden Goose.

The Golden Goose claimed to be the oldest of the houses along the Lucky Strike. Its name supported the claim, harking back to a time when gold was valuable, before the superabundance of that metal on Dorado undermined its value for ever.

It was built of solid gold, which even now produced a feeling of opulence, as if customers could never quite shake off their racial inheritance of gold fever. The people who patronised it were amongst the richest in Gold City.

Sarn gritted his teeth as he entered the plush portal, knowing full well that minimum stakes in the Golden Goose were the highest on the whole of the Lucky Strike.

As he laid bets against the random number generator, he spied a woman watching him with an air of amusement. He glanced at her. She had long golden hair, her skin was powdered with gold, and her gold thread dress fell to the floor in expensive folds. Her arms and shoulders were bare. Tiny stars were painted across her forehead, and on her head she wore a circlet of chromium. At her throat she wore a miniature portrait which, if it was genuine, would make her a walking bank account.

He turned away from the machine and returned her smile.

'It's not my lucky night!' he said ruefully.

'Nor mine!' laughed the woman. 'I've given up playing, but it's nearly as much fun just watching.'

'Do you often just watch?' asked Denson.

'Quite often,' admitted the golden blonde.

'Perhaps you've noticed a friend of mine,' said the Tec. 'His name's Jaimi Borrowitch . . . '

The woman's eyes became watchful.

'Is he really a friend of yours?' she asked quietly. Denson realised she was not the empty-head she appeared at first sight. There was obviously a limit to the extent to which he would be able to fool her. He fell back on a second line of prevarication.

'Well no,' he admitted. 'Not personally. More a friend of a friend really. This friend is worried about him — hasn't seen him for a while. He asked me to keep an eye open for him.'

'Can't the friend do his own looking?' asked the blonde, still wary.

'Not in here he can't!' replied Denson cheerfully. 'He's not exactly welcome in these establishments any more.'

The woman relaxed. 'That figures,' she acknowledged brightly. 'A friend of Jaimi's would quite likely be afflicted that way.'

'He wanted me to check up,' said Denson.

'You're not really a gambler yourself?'

'No, I'm only here to oblige a friend.'

'It's a shame about Jaimi. I liked him. He was good fun to have around, but a bad loser I guess.'

'Perhaps he'll find the money to meet his obligations in due course ... ' ventured the Tec.

'It'll make no difference if he does,' said the woman, a little sadly. 'Once you default the big boys, they never forgive and they never forget. There's nowhere on Dorado that would let Jaimi play again.'

'Sad,' commented Denson.

'Too bad,' agreed the blonde. 'If your

friend wants to find him, he'd best look at the Borrowitch column. There's nowhere else Jaimi would be welcome right now.'

'I guess you're right,' agreed Sarn. 'I'll tell him that.'

'No hurry is there?' enquired the woman, arching her brows. 'I'm not much of a gambler myself. Perhaps we could go and find some more congenial occupation.'

The Tec was sorely tempted, but had to admit to himself that it would look extremely odd on an expense account, should he ever get to placing one.

'You're not his brother, are you?' asked the woman, while Denson was still casting about in his mind for a polite brush-off. He was startled. 'No. Why do you ask?'

The woman shrugged her beautiful golden shoulders, accentuating the effect of her low-cut dress. 'I don't know. He was always talking about his brother — seems to have become some sort of paragon — just the sort of guy to come looking for Jaimi if he was to go missing.'

'Jaimi didn't like his brother?' asked the Tec.

'You ask an awful lot of questions,' smiled the woman. 'I'm not answering any more — unless you buy me a drink in some cosy little tavern . . . '

Denson changed his mind about the expense account. It would stand a drink at any rate, he thought. The woman took Denson's arm as they left the complex, and laid her head lightly on his shoulder.

'My name's Seelya Koto,' she said.

'Sarn Denson,' grunted the Tec.

They strolled along the boulevard, and then turned into a narrow side street, lit with coloured lanterns and crowded with people. Tavern signs projected above almost every doorway, and the smell of alcohol threatened to drown Seelya's provocative perfume.

'Let's try this one,' she said, and pulled him through an arched portal into a dimly lit, cellar-like room. It was divided into a number of tiny booths by wooden partitions which provided an illusion of seclusion.

The proprietor, a squat pale individual who looked as if he hailed from Deneb, brought them a thick green wine made from berries native to Dorado, and laced with a Denebian spice. Denson sipped it gingerly, uncomfortably aware of the potency of the wine and the supposed aphrodisiac properties of the spice.

Seelya's eyes sparkled as she lifted her own glass. The Tec returned somewhat reluctantly to business.

'You were going to tell me if Jaimi disliked his brother . . . ' he reminded her.

'Was I?' she fenced. She thought. 'I don't think he did really. He pretended to, but I think it was just a pose. He was the younger brother, you see, trying to compensate for some sense of inferiority.'

'Are you a psychiatrist?' enquired Denson curiously.

'No, just interested. I'm interested in most things to do with people. That's why Jaimi Borrowitch entertained me. It wasn't so much that he was interesting in himself, but that he came from such an intriguing family. Do you know the family very well?'

'Not intimately,' parried the Tec.

'You know about Adelin Borrowitch and Nadya Lasolere, of course . . . ?'

Fortunately she didn't wait for Denson to reply, but went on talking about how fascinating it was, and gradually the Tec pieced the story together. He began to feel very grateful to Seelya. To think he had gone to that repulsive hulk Effel Sternbloom for information that he was now receiving from the delectable Miss Koto. He was so absorbed in the information — and its source — that he forgot his qualms about the liquor and ordered more.

There was music coming from a neighbouring tavern, and Seelya suggested they danced. So one thing led to another, and the Tec finished up knowing a great deal more about Seelya Koto than was strictly relevant to his enquiries . . .

6

Family of a Bizman

It was late the next morning when Sarn Denson left Seelya Koto's module, and he was feeling a bit worn. He drove carefully along the city's outer circle cable until he reached the cableway which wound up into the hills.

Shatter Hill was one of the highest of the outlying suburbs, and so was one of the most exclusive. The pylons were tall and looked like giant flowers with modules clustered like buds at their tips. The hill was thickly wooded, and the columns protruded from clumps of dense foliage. They were widely separated, indicating that the ground attached to each was considerable.

The Tec found the turn-off to the Borrowitch pylon, and his car began to grind up the steep cable, along an avenue cut through the trees. The hawser curved to the right, and then back to the left, cutting off the view of the company cableway. Abruptly he was out in a clearing and ahead of him the pylon reared skyward. There was garaging at ground level, built to avoid the ugly tracery of cables climbing the column, and Denson slid his car into one of the several berths marked 'Visitor'. At the rear of the garage was a door into a corridor leading to a lift.

Denson pressed a button to summon an elevator. When it arrived and the doors slid open, the Tec saw it was occupied by a tall still man in a dark uniform.

'May I ask your name and business please, sir?' asked the man courteously. There was something about the voice that puzzled Sarn.

'I'm Tec Denson, and I've come to see Jaimi Borrowitch.'

'I don't believe he's expecting you, sir,' was the reply in the curiously flat, monotonously polite intonation.

'When somebody is murdered, everyone connected with them expects to talk to a Tec sooner or later!' snapped Denson.

'Of course. Will you excuse me one

moment while I consult?'

The man stood perfectly still. He was so still that the Tec observed him intently, wondering what it was that was nagging at the edge of his consciousness. The servant must be using a sub-vocal communicator — but no, not even his throat muscles moved, and there was no sign of any other movement. The man didn't even blink. Of course, thought Sarn, he must be a domestic robot, and a simulated human at that, which showed how rich the Bizman must have been.

The robot smiled primly.

'You will be admitted,' it said.

Denson resisted the impulse to thank the machine, and instead stepped into the elevator. A minute later he was standing in the corridor which led to Jaimi Borrowitch's module. He strode up to the door and pressed the centre button with his thumb, staring straight at the electronic eye which glared at him from the upper middle of the door. The door swung open and the Tec entered.

He found himself in a colourful room, where slabs of primaries tapestried the walls, complemented by a deep blue carpet, deep both in pile and colour. Bright yellow curtains hung by the windows, and in the centre of the room floated a luminous orange globe. Jaimi Borrowitch lounged on a bright red day bed, his eyes on a large viewer which spread across a third of one wall between violet and green drapes. A naked girl danced sensuously across the glowing screen, and froze in the exact centre, her body arched back, arms flung wide and legs apart, as Jaimi stilled the tape. He regarded it reflectively for a moment, before the curtains swished across the screen, and he turned to look at Denson. It was another protracted interval before he seemed to register the Tec's existence. The scent of tobacco proclaimed Jaimi's addiction to the drug.

'What do you want?' he demanded rudely.

'I want to talk to you,' replied Denson, his voice expressionless.

'I've already told all I know to that numb-skull buddy of yours — what's his name?'

'Garwen,' supplied Sarn, happy once again to be mistaken for an employee of City Investigators. 'The office wasn't too impressed with his report. Our fault really; we oughtn't to have sent someone as insensitive as Garwen to interview a man of taste and refinement such as yourself.'

Denson mentally thanked Seelya for the lowdown she'd given him on Jaimi's self-delusions.

'Yes. He was a bit crude,' responded Jaimi. 'He seemed to have no appreciation of the artistic way of life. I'm blasted if he didn't actually look disapproving when I told him of my gambling problems.'

Sarn clicked his tongue sympathetically. 'Did you decorate this room yourself?' he asked.

'Yes. You like it?' asked Jaimi.

'Sure thing,' said the Tec, 'especially the mobile on the wall.'

'Huh?' Jaimi looked puzzled for a minute. 'Oh, you mean the tape! Yes, good isn't she? A friend in Joy City sent it to me. Couldn't get for myself, of course. Those gambling boyos have put the mockers on my credit ratings over the whole blasted planet.'

'You'll be all right, though, once your father's estate is settled . . . ?' reminded the Tec.

Jaimi brightened visibly. 'That's true. Even when it's divided up, the old man's lot should go quite a long way.'

'Of course, it might be suggested that you'd rather more to gain from his death than was healthy for the Bizman.'

'What the hell do you mean by that?' blustered the Bizman's son. 'I thought you people had Ros Kernwell lined up for the rap.'

'City Investigators have no doubt that Accountant Kernwell was the culprit,' replied the Tec smoothly, 'but the accused may fall back on the well-tried trick of flying a few saucers. After all, if her counsel can show that other people had motives for the Bizman's murder, the computer may well refuse to deliver a verdict in the first instance. At present, there's very little hard evidence against her.'

'Well, anyone who tries to pin anything

on me will have their work cut out,' spat Jaimi. 'I've a very substantial Accused Person Policy.'

'Paid for by your father of course,' commented Denson.

'Sure it is. Dad had his head screwed on tightly where money was concerned, even if he was a bit Earth-bound in other ways. All our insurance premiums are paid from a trust fund separate from his business and personal estate, so his death doesn't affect the payments. All of us are fully covered for as long as we live.'

'All of you?' interposed Denson.

'Me, Zarah, Obert and Adelin.'

'Not Nadya?'

Jaimi looked genuinely puzzled. 'No, of course not! Nadya isn't one of the family. She's just a friend of Adelin's. Dad wouldn't waste his money on someone like that.'

'You seem well informed about his financial arrangements yourself,' probed the Tec.

'Dad made sure we knew what cover we had, so as we'd know what to do in a jam.'

Sarn rose. 'So you've nothing to worry about . . . '

'Not me!' grinned Jaimi. 'Just as soon as the money comes through, I'll be as free as a space-bug! I can't wait to get back to the bright lights and the number machines. I'm fed up with life at second hand. Now, if you've finished, I'll get back to my viewing . . . '

'I may be back,' said Denson as he left.

He sighed. Pity he couldn't have stayed to see the rest of the tape. It looked a good deal more interesting than life at first hand.

He pondered the interview. Jaimi was obviously a suspect, but there was nothing but motive. It was interesting about Nadya Lasolere. Evidently the Bizman hadn't bought out the gossip about her for her own sake, but simply to protect his wife. He wondered if Effel Sternbloom had come up with the same story Seelya had given him. He supposed he'd have to go and find out sooner or later, if only to keep on the right side of her — it was a vast side after all. In the meantime, there were other members of the Borrowitch family to see.

When the lift door opened, the robot was waiting for him.

'I'd like to see Obert Borrowitch now,' instructed the Tec brusquely.

'I regret to say he is not in,' replied the robot.

'Then I'll speak to Zarah.'

'I regret to say she is not in either.'

'Is there anyone else at home?' asked Denson, knowing that acerbity would be wasted on the robot, but venting his feelings anyway.

'Adelin Borrowitch is at home.'

'May I see her then, if you don't mind?' requested Sarn sarcastically.

'I will enquire.'

There was a momentary silence, before the robot said, 'I will take you to her.'

★   ★   ★

The Bizman's widow was dressed in a black jump-suit which emphasised her pallor. Nevertheless, she had considerable beauty, and Denson was impressed.

'I must apologise for troubling you in

your grief,' he began sincerely, 'but there are still some matters which need clarification.'

'Of course, Tec Denson, I quite understand.'

Sarn Denson had enjoyed deceiving Jaimi Borrowitch over his true commitment, but he felt uncomfortable about imposing the deception on this woman, who was so obviously distressed. However, he told himself, it was his duty, and he ploughed on.

'You know, of course, that Ros Kernwell is the prime suspect in this case. However, the evidence against her is largely circumstantial. If she is astutely defended, the defence may be able to direct suspicions towards other people, and thus reduce the probabilities of the various factors against her. To guard against this, it is necessary to be able to refute any suspicions, so that they may instead be assigned a low probability.'

'I do understand the basis of the law machines' functions,' murmured Adelin Borrowitch.

'Of course,' acknowledged the Tec.

'Well then, you will see that we must be certain no case can be made out against anyone else — even, shall we say, yourself . . . '

The Bizman's wife said nothing, but Denson thought he detected a sudden wariness in her eyes.

'There has been a certain amount of gossip about you — gossip which your husband bought out of the records. He couldn't prevent it from continuing, of course, but he did what he could to expunge it from the data banks.'

Still Adelin said nothing.

'I know what the gossip was,' continued Denson softly, 'and, if it is true, it would appear that you might have a motive for wishing your husband dead.'

'All that was a long time ago,' sighed Adelin Borrowitch. 'I no longer have any interest in it.'

'I believe you,' said the Tec. 'You were not the only one involved, of course.'

'You mean Nadya?'

Sarn nodded. 'Do you think she wishes to forget as totally as you do?'

Adelin hesitated. 'Perhaps you could

ask her that,' she suggested.

'Your husband deleted the gossip concerning her too,' Denson went on. 'Was that at her request?'

'He did that simply because Nadya and I were — are — friends. It was to protect me.'

The Tec changed the subject abruptly, watching Adelin as he spoke: 'I had hoped to see Obert, but he isn't here today.'

Did he detect a slight reddening of Adelin's countenance? She and Obert were not so different in age. If there was any attachment between them, that would constitute a powerful motive for either to murder the Bizman.

'Obert is seldom here,' observed Adelin. 'He is very much involved with the Brotherhood of Earth.'

'Really?' asked Denson, intrigued as always by a link with the cradle of Mankind. 'He has not joined the Brotherhood, I take it?'

'No, but he used to talk about doing so.'

'He doesn't any more?'

'Edlin forbade it. They quarrelled

rather bitterly about it all, and after that Obert never spoke of the Brotherhood again, but he remained involved in their work.'

'And did the Bizman know that?'

Adelin nodded.

'What had your husband got against the Brotherhood of Earth? They seem harmless, and they do a lot of good for those who are destitute.'

'Edlin said their charity could get out of hand, that it could undermine the commercial ethos of Dorado. If people believed that the Brotherhood would care for them, feed them and clothe them if they lost all their money, then people would give up trying. Why should people work if they could get necessities free? Besides, Edlin suspected that the Brotherhood collected far more money from the citizens of Dorado than they spent here. The surplus, he believed, was sent to their missions on other worlds. They were draining capital from Dorado to support otherworlders.

'He couldn't explain why that should be necessary, since most civilised planets except Dorado have state welfare systems. Sometimes he even accused the Brotherhood of being a subversive operation of Earth Government, deliberately sucking the life-blood of the star worlds and infusing it into the hardened arteries of Earth's creaking mercantile system. After all, they all face Sol when they pray.'

As Adelin Borrowitch spoke, Denson felt he was hearing the words of Edlin Borrowitch, not his wife. The Brotherhood was a subject on which the Bizman must have expounded often, so that his wife had come to know his views word for word.

Adelin looked thoughtful. 'That was what Edlin used to say, but I don't think that was the true cause of his bitterness. I never heard him denounce the Brotherhood before Obert became involved with them. I think it was anger over Obert's betrayal of the commercial ethic that upset Edlin. He was disappointed when Obert made it plain that he had no intention of continuing his training to take command of Edlin's business empire — indeed, he once said that whatever

98

came to him, he would sell and use the proceeds for the cause of the Brotherhood. Edlin had determined that Obert should succeed him, as he always seemed so much more reliable and steady than Jaimi. After Obert's defection, Edlin didn't know what to do for the best. He hadn't the patience to wait and see if Obert's conversion was but a passing whim.'

Adelin paused. The analysis of her husband's motives had seized her interest, and she was probing more deeply into them. The Tec sat patiently, unmoving, making no sound. Adelin's monologue was telling him more about the stresses in the Borrowitch household than he might learn from a hundred questions.

'There was a more basic concern, however, than the fate of his trading empire. The Brotherhood make vows of celibacy.'

Sarn nodded in understanding.

'Edlin had always counted on Obert carrying on the Borrowitch line,' she went on. 'Because of that, I think he had neglected Jaimi somewhat — allowed him to go his own way too much. Now he felt it was too late to reclaim Jaimi for the more serious duties of life. There was always Zarah, of course, but Edlin was old-fashioned about women. He would prefer to hand down his empire via the male line.'

Adelin smiled briefly, and the passage of the smile transformed her face into a picture of dazzling beauty.

'At one stage, Edlin became so overwrought about it all, he even suggested that I should have a son by him, just to give him a new heir.'

The Tec could not resist intervening at last. 'Was that so surprising?' he asked.

Adelin hesitated. 'The difference in our ages is quite large. If we had had a child, Edlin would have been old before it was even half grown. Besides, I don't want any children — and just imagine the jealousy it would have provoked in the family. No, it would have been quite an impracticable solution.'

'Did the Bizman resent your refusal?' asked Sarn.

Adelin looked surprised. 'No! I think he realised himself that it wasn't a sensible idea.'

'There's just one other thing,' said Denson. 'Did your husband ever have any business enemies? Rivals, perhaps, that he had previously put out of business?'

'Of course. All successful Bizmen have many enemies — that must be obvious, surely?'

'Can you think of anybody in particular?' persisted the Tec.

'I don't really know. I never enquired much about his work. I'm just not interested in it. In any case, it is not one's enemies that are dangerous — one is automatically cautious of enemies, so one can usually either avoid or outmanoeuvre them. It is friends who are the danger — people one trusts.'

'Friends and family . . . ' said Denson. He stood up. 'Thank you. You have been both patient and helpful.'

At the door he turned. 'Do you know where I might find Zarah?'

Adelin shrugged. 'She'll be with Arick Earthborn, I don't doubt. You might try the studios, but they could be anywhere really.'

★   ★   ★

As Denson piloted his car off the Borrowitch cable on to the intercity wire, he puzzled over the interviews he had had with Adelin and Jaimi. Practically all of the family had a motive for killing the Bizman — Jaimi because he needed his inheritance, Obert because he wanted to lead his own life, Adelin because her husband might have pressed her harder about having a child than she had admitted, Nadya Lasolere because she and Adelin thought that Borrowitch's death might give them both the freedom to pursue their designs. There was no evidence, however.

Denson decided he would call in and see Effel Sternbloom in case she knew anything more than he had learned from Seelya, and then he would pay a visit to Nadya Lasolere . . .

7

Nadya Lasolere

Sarn Denson learnt nothing from his visit to Effel Sternbloom, but in case he should need her help another time, he forced himself to be suitably grateful to her, and endured her grotesque coquetries as long as he could. He refused her offer of liquid refreshment, but availed himself of the nearest tavern as soon as he was able to escape, and there fortified himself with a stiff slug of fodya from Merak 21.

Nadya Lasolere inhabited a quarter of the city which had a Bohemian reputation. (The Tec was rather proud of the fact that he knew the origin of the adjective 'Bohemian', having come across the word while reading a popular work on the ancient history of the Sol system). The columns crowded close to the cableways, and jostled each other for module space, with the result that only the smallest of modules could be accomodated. Few of them retained their propulsion units in working order, so that they had in fact become permanent dwellings in an area originally designed for a migratory population, to whom cramped accomodation would not be unsuitable.

As he drove carefully along the narrow chasm between the heavily loaded pylons, he saw below him a dark patch of swiftly moving shadow. It sped down the street and then turned aside, and then he realised it to be a horde of cats, those enigmatic creatures introduced from Earth long ago.

There was a legend that they had been brought to Dorado by a fortune hunter, one Dik Ritting, who had heard that the early colonists were at their wits end on account of the indigenous rodent population, which was feeding voraciously on anything the farmers tried to cultivate. Ritting's cats had savaged the rodent population, but had rapidly got out of hand themselves, living in the wild and scavenging in the cities. But the pioneers had been grateful to Ritting and rewarded him so richly that he was able to found a great merchant house. It was a charming tale, loved by children, but alas there was no evidence to support it. The House of Ritting, if it had ever existed, had vanished completely. The cats, however, were still here, wild and fierce, enigmatic and unapproachable.

Denson located Nadya's column, and parked his car on the communal cable which served the occupants of the pylon. He took the lift to the seventeenth bracket and walked along the corridor to the fifth hatchway. He pressed the button and waited. He recognised the door as being of one-way laminate, so he assumed a reassuring demeanour, hoping to allay any suspicions Nadya Lasolere might have.

The door spoke to him. It had a pleasant voice, but not yet a welcoming one: 'Who are you and what is your business?'

'I'm Tec Sarn Denson, and would like to talk to you about the circumstances surrounding the death of Bizman Edlin Borrowitch.'

'I've already been interviewed by Tec Garwen,' replied the door.

'There are still more angles that need opening out,' explained Denson patiently.

'Show me your guild card.'

Denson held up his card at the blank door, certain now that it was one-way transparent.

'You're not with City Investigators,' the door accused.

'I didn't say I was,' replied Denson. 'I just said I wanted to talk to you about the case.'

'Whose interests do you represent?'

'That doesn't make any difference to the facts of the case, and that is what I'm interested in.'

'Well I've nothing to say to you,' decided the door with an air of finality.

'Look,' argued the Tec, 'I hate to play rough, but I know all about yours and Adelin's youthful preoccupations. It's not the sort of stuff you'd like to have come out at a trial, and go into the law files. I don't want that to happen either, so I'm giving you the chance to clear things up now, informally. If you refuse, however, you'll leave me no choice.'

The door faded away, dissolving into a picture of a beautiful but angry woman.

'Come in,' spat Nadya Lasolere.

Denson stepped across the threshold and the door reformed behind him.

The woman was wearing a lounging dress. From the belted waist it was slit down each side to reveal long legs, and up at the front, only partially concealing pointed breasts. She turned, and Denson saw that the back of her dress matched the front, plunging almost to the base of the spine. Her long dark hair was a black cascade against the white skin. Nadya Lasolere moved to a low couch and half lay on it, her long legs crossed. She gestured to an upright chair cast from gold, hard and uncomfortable even for one of Denson's fitness. Her beautiful face with its high cheekbones and heavily shaded eyes was set and unfriendly.

'Well?' queried the woman, raising pencilled eyebrows towards blue-black hair.

Denson stared across the room and through the open window at the azure sky, a sky as blue as the heavens of Earth. He spoke softly, almost dreamily:

'You and Adelin were mixed up in a political movement called Protection for the People. It was one of those impractical dreams born of youthful enthusiasm to build a better world. It advocated re-introducing the concept of government to Dorado. You planned to set up a bureaucracy to regulate the companies and all commercial enterprises. The bureaucracy would be financed by the levying of taxes on businesses. As well as regulations, it was proposed that welfare should be made available to the improvident. In short, you preached a revolution that would turn Dorado into a corporate state like Alshain Three or Hamal Seven.'

Denson turned his sombre gaze on the beautiful woman who was now standing half turned away from him, towards the windows.

'Nothing criminal,' he went on, 'perhaps even praiseworthy. It depends on your point of view, and I'm not blind to the defects that exist in the social set up here on Dorado. But not the sort of views that make you popular with people like Bizman Borrowitch.'

Nadya Lasolere turned towards him. 'I don't care if you do rake all that out in public,' she said with quiet hatred. 'It's not going to do your client any good, but if you get a kick out of it, go ahead. I wouldn't expect any different from a louse.'

'It isn't quite as simple as that,' persisted Denson patiently. 'There isn't any hard evidence against Ros Kernwell. All that City Investigators have is a motive. They're digging around for evidence, but I believe Ros Kernwell is innocent, so I don't think they're going to find any. Nevertheless, motive would probably be sufficient to give her a conviction — unless anyone else had a credible motive. Both you and Adelin had — or at least, it is believable that you had.'

'Really?' sneered Nadya. 'Borrowitch knew all about my beliefs. There's no motive there.'

'Adelin obviously abandoned her commitment to Protection for the People, maybe for Borrowitch's sake. I don't know. But suppose her interest revived?'

'Suppose it did?' snapped Nadya. 'Husbands and wives are allowed to have different opinions, aren't they?'

'You'd be surprised how often they kill each other just because they don't see eye to eye,' replied the Tec morosely.

'Even a cynical slob like you can see Adelin would be incapable of murdering anyone. If she couldn't stick Borrowitch any longer, she might have left him, but she'd never have done him physical harm.'

'But if she left him, she'd be creditless,' objected the Tec, 'and if — I only say if — her interest in Protection for the People revived, she might be tempted to get hold of his wealth to use for the cause.'

'You're mad if you think that!' interrupted Nadya.

'It doesn't really matter what I think,' countered Denson. 'It's what the computer calculates that counts, and the law machines don't take innocent looks into consideration. Evidence, motive and opportunity are the things the Justices are programmed to weigh up.'

There was an unfriendly silence.

'Of course, there are other possibilities,' murmured Sarn. He coughed, almost apologetically. 'Consider your own position, for instance.'

Nadya Lasolere shifted uneasily and stared at him intently. Denson found her proximity disturbing, and strove to concentrate his thoughts.

'Supposing you retained your allegiance to the movement throughout. You might have harboured a festering grudge against the Bizman for seducing Adelin from the cause — not enough to murder perhaps, not after all this time. Yet suppose further that you saw Adelin's faith reviving. You might have calculated that, with Borrowitch dead, you'd be able to win back Adelin's commitment, and with it wealth she would have inherited to provide finance for your dreams.'

'Too many suppositions, no proof. Too many ifs, no evidence,' jeered Nadya. 'You couldn't make that stick in a million years.'

'I'm not interested in making it stick,' replied the Tec. 'All I need to do is provide sufficient doubt, enough of an alternative, to reduce Ros Kernwell's probability rating below the conviction level. I think if I work on it, dig a bit deeper into what you and Adelin did in the past, then I'll be able to present a cohesive case against one or the other of you — a case good enough to raise reasonable doubt.'

Nadya Lasolere leaned forward, and the effect on her already inadequate clothing was devastating. Denson's discomfort became almost intolerable.

'How is Ros Kernwell paying you?' she asked softly. 'She hasn't been charged, so she must have hired you direct. I know Ros. She has no money — not unless she's guilty, of course. But you don't believe she's guilty, do you?'

Sarn shook his head — his throat was too dry for speech.

'Then she can't have paid you any credit. She has only one other thing to give — herself. Is that how it is?'

Again the Tec shook his head.

'I don't really want you raking up my past, or Adelin's' Nadya went on. 'You won't find anything that will help Ros, but you may agitate painful memories. If you leave these stones unturned, I should regard that as an act of chivalry on your part, and I find chivalry irresistable.'

Denson closed his eyes and thought of Seelya. Abruptly he stood up. Nadya Lasolere straightened her body, and stared up at him from her large dark eyes.

'Don't tell me chivalry is so dead that even the offer of a grateful damsel can't revive it!' she said sardonically.

The Tec found his voice at last. 'If it is possible for me to spare you and Adelin the distress, I shall do so, but my first duty is to my client. I shall do whatever is necessary to save her.'

Nadya Lasolere pursed her lips petulantly, and raised a white shoulder in a dismissive shrug. 'You're a fool,' she commented.

★   ★   ★

As Sarn Denson recrossed the city, he found himself agreeing with Nadya Lasolere. He seldom met any woman quite so exotic as she, and only once in a ringless moon have the chance of bedding one. Why had he passed up the chance? If he'd accepted her invitation, it needn't have influenced his investigation at all. If she believed it would, then she herself was no more than a fool. Perhaps he was just inadequate, he told himself bitterly.

He jostled his car across the main Hinterland Expressway feeder wires from the Coast Boulevard, and joined the city's southern suburban route. Settled into the medium fast lane, he tried to raise Ros Kernwell on Person-to-Person, but there was no reply.

A tiny seed of foreboding germinated. There was no reason why she shouldn't have left the city limits, but he couldn't think of a good reason why she should, and there were a number of possible bad reasons.

His irrational fears were clothed in rationality by a call from Garwen. Denson accepted the call, and the visage of his rival grew bright on his screen. Keeping one eye on the ugly physiognomy of the big bureau investigator, and the other on the cableway, Sarn listened to the other Tec's jeering enquiries.

'Seen your client lately?' asked Garwen, with an air of one knowing the answer.

'None of your business!' snapped Denson.

'I suppose you didn't know she'd skipped?' Garwen went on.

Sarn said nothing, but felt a sinking feeling in the pit of his stomach.

'Not very smart of you to let her do that,' sneered Garwen. 'Evidence of flight will push the guilt probability way up, and it was already set to be pretty high.'

'That's all bluff,' snarled Denson, but he knew it wasn't — not the remark about Evidence of Flight anyway.

'Of course, if you didn't know about it, it's even worse,' probed Garwen. 'It'll make you look pretty silly either way, but if she's skedaddled without consulting you, it probably means she can't pay you either.'

'There'll be plenty of money as soon as

she's charged,' countered Denson.

'That's a pretty defeatist attitude,' gloated Garwen. 'Anyway, there's no guarantee you'll get any of it, is there? It'll be up to the company to whom the policy is assigned to appoint an investigator, and they're hardly likely to choose you, after you've made such a mess of things so far.'

Denson knew Garwen was right. He resisted the impulse to wipe the smug face from his screen — Garwen might let slip some scrap of information, and Sarn was desperate for a lead.

'Well, I'll be signing off now,' announced Garwen, as if he'd read Denson's thought. 'Here's hoping you find a more profitable assignment next time!'

The image faded, but that last remark had kindled a spark of hope in Denson. Why had Garwen called him? There was only one matter of substance in their conversation, and that was Garwen telling him that Ros Kernwell had fled. Assuming it was true, why had Garwen told him? It could only be in the hope that Denson would throw in his hand and retire from the case. Garwen's final comment confirmed that analysis. That meant City Investigators still hadn't got a cast iron case. They were worried that Denson might dig up something to upset the probabilities. Ergo, it was worth continuing. What was more, Garwen's clumsy attempt at arousing Denson's commercial instincts gave him the determination to suppress them, and to battle on whether he got paid or not.

Sarn Denson moved from the medium fast wire to the high speed cable, and his car hummed along the outskirts of Gold City. The Brotherhood of Earth had its retreat just outside the city boundary, on a tract of land that had somehow remained unclaimed for centuries after the settlement. With their unerring instinct for minimising expenditure and maximising income, the Brothers had discovered that the land was ownerless, and had promptly registered a claim with Property Agency Unlimited, the monopoly conveyancing combine.

Leaving behind the last of the residential pylons, the cableway swung westward across a jumbled landscape, but Denson took an easterly spur, a double-stranded route with overtaking loops which wound perilously close to the ground.

The cableway was a new one, erected by the Brotherhood for the convenience of its lay following, those adherents who could not bring themselves to renounce their old way of life, yet felt compelled to offer some sacrifice to the religion which was slowly spreading among the civilised worlds.

Rounding a final cliff, Denson brought the cable car to an involuntary halt. In front of him stretched meadows of green grass and yellow flowers, undulating over the former dunes of the coastal plain, azure speckled with gold by the afternoon sun. Close by the shore rose a majestic pile.

Tower upon buttressed tower, spire upon steepled spire, the retreat of the Brotherhood of Earth scrambled towards the heavens, as if eager to return to the planet of Man's birth . . .

8

The Brotherhood of Earth

The Tec restarted the car and rode smoothly across the sun-drenched fields. The habitat of the brethren glowed rose red in Aurum's golden light. The cable took him to a quay near the foot of the castle.

Climbing out of the car, he left it there and crossed to a flight of rough-hewn steps which led to a door of tough leathery wood that came from the weeds of the coastal seas. The flat metallic plate of an identity screen was set in the stone arch of the doorway. Denson pressed his hand on it, and waited as the electronic watchdog combed its memory for any record of his being an undesirable person, according to whatever definition of desirable the Brotherhood had stipulated to the screening company. It seemed that Tecs were not on the unwanted list, for the door swung silently inward and he went through.

He was met by a smiling brother in a green and blue robe, who came forward with outstretched hands. Rather self-consciously, Denson took them, and found his own were affectionately squeezed.

'Welcome to our refuge,' intoned the man in a sing-song voice. 'Whatever has brought you here serves Gaia's purpose.'

'Gaia?' replied Sarn quizzically.

'The Earth Goddess,' explained the brother. 'The living embodiment of the planet of our origin. She watches over Her children wherever they may be. However far from Her they may wander, in space or in spirit, She is with them, and will bring them safe home at last.'

'Yes,' interrupted Denson hastily, hoping to forestall what was obviously going to be a fairly lengthy sales pitch. 'I'm not here on my own account. I'm looking for a man named Obert Borrowitch.'

The brother gave a poor imitation of inscrutability.

'We are not concerned with such matters,' he ventured loftily.

'This isn't all that mundane,' rasped the Tec. 'His father has been murdered and an innocent woman is being accused.'

The man flinched perceptibly. 'What part do you play in these unhappy events?' he asked.

Denson explained with as much patience as he could muster.

'I need to talk to Obert,' he finished, 'to give me another angle on the whole business.'

'It is true that Comrade Obert was here,' admitted the brother reluctantly. 'He seemed set to become a novice of our order. Then yesterday he was visited by a colleague of yours.'

'A Tec?' interrupted Sarn.

The brother nodded, and when Denson described Garwen to him, agreed that it was he.

'They spoke briefly, and then Comrade Obert announced that he would be leaving immediately.' A note of disapproval frosted the brother's next remark. 'He said he was going to Joy City.'

Denson suppressed a grin. He reckoned a few days of the Brotherhood would be enough to send him hightailing to Joy City too. Then he was brought up short by the remembrance that Ros Kernwell had also fled. Could there be any connection? Had Garwen told Obert more than he had told Denson?

Or did Obert have another source of information? Either way, it was the first inkling he had of where Ros might have gone if she really had left the city. It also made him more anxious than ever to interview Obert.

'Thanks,' he said to the brother. 'I won't waste any more of your time.'

'You have wasted none,' replied the man gravely. 'If you return, you will be welcome.'

Denson nodded and walked back to his car.

The sun was hot, and the gentle breeze blowing up from the sea was welcome. He opened the windows of the car and eased it away from the quay. Soon he was speeding back towards the main cable-way, enjoying the cool of the slipstream. As he entered the rocky area, he slowed, and began to feel hot again as he followed the twisting route. Rounding a bend, he entered a short length of straight wire, at the end of which was a stationary car. He slowed still further and sounded his siren. Nothing happened. He touched a button and, in one small square of his front screen, the other car leapt closer. At this high magnification, it was plainly empty.

The Tec stopped his own vehicle, perplexed and suspicious. It was this suspicion, together with a slight movement caught by his exceptionally wide-angled vision, and the fact that the side windows of his car were open to catch the wind of his passage, that combined to save his life. The tiny movement made him duck instinctively, and an explosive pellet whined in at one window of his car, and out at the other. It struck the opposite cliff with a thunderous detonation. The cable car rocked from side to side with the blast of the explosion, and Denson might easily have been dashed against the steel bodywork had he not been securely strapped in.

Without raising his head, he poked at buttons on the control panel, and, as the cable car went into reverse at high speed, he prayed that no one had set off from the retreat in his wake. If the ambusher had a confederate at Denson's rear, then he was finished.

The car swerved violently to one side, and Denson knew he was out of the defile. He brought the vehicle to a standstill and cautiously peered over the fascia. He waited. Nothing happened. Crouching on the floor of his car, he inched it forward, peeping over the solidity of the control board at intervals. When he re-entered the straight, he found it empty. His unknown assailant must have regained the car and made off. Nevertheless, he proceeded with circumspection in case the disappearance of the other car was but a further ruse.

He reached the end of the straight and stole round the next bend. After several twists, he was back on a longer straight stretch, just in time to see the other car disappearing into the woods. It was then that he had his biggest piece of luck in the whole episode. Or perhaps his subconscious was working overtime. Certainly he was suspicious that the other car had moved so slowly that he had caught up with it despite his own slow pace. Was he wary that he might be being tempted towards destruction? Whatever the reason, he slowed to a halt and hesitated about his next move. So he was safely on an independently suspended section of cable, when the next section, the stretch along which he would have been moving if he had not stopped, suddenly went limp and crashed to the ground.

The would-be assassin must have severed the cable, bringing down the whole length from one isolating pylon to the next. Denson would almost certainly have been killed or crippled if he'd been travelling along it at the time. He'd seen enough victims of accidental cable breaks to cause him to shudder at the thought of the fate he had so miraculously avoided. His adversary was obviously quite ruthless and resourceful, and the Tec would need all his faculties to defeat him.

Denson contacted the cable company and informed them of the failure, but not of his suspicions as to the cause, and then took his car back to the retreat. Driving slowly and carefully, he moved his car up the approach wire, hoping there would be no other visitor to the brothers until he had regained the main cableway. He passed the collapsed section, but from his car he could see no clues, and he had no time to waste on a closer inspection.

The Tec returned to his office. He thought for a bit and then called Adelin Borrowitch.

'Was there anything between your Obert and Ros Kernwell?' he asked. Adelin considered for a moment.

'I know that Jaimi was interested in her at one time,' she said, 'but I don't know about Obert. Lately, at any rate, he had no time for anything except the Brotherhood.'

'Did Jaimi and Ros have a serious relationship?' enquired the Tec.

'I shouldn't think so,' answered Adelin unhesitantly. 'Jaimi pursues girls compulsively, just as he gambles. I think Ros was far too sensible to fall for his sort of approach.'

'Did Jaimi ever make advances towards

you?' ventured Denson.

'I've answered enough of your questions,' replied Adelin quietly. 'I have done all I can to help you, and I'm sure I know nothing more of use to you. Since you seem determined to pursue your inquiry along impertinent, even obscene, lines, I have nothing more to say.'

She faded from view, and the Tec was left with an impression of dignified outrage. He smiled ruefully to himself. There were some things about being a Tec that he didn't much care for.

He leaned back, and his chair swivelled away from the desk and unfolded, so that he lay comfortably on his back staring at the ceiling. A reproduction of Cananzan-otti's 'Galaxy' spread across the room in black, flecked with a myriad of hued pinpoints. Denson sighed and let his imagination drift towards the outer reaches of deep space. He wondered how it would feel to be a disembodied intelligence, free to wing across the void between the stars and bathe in their fierce radiation. To watch, silent and alone, as the Universe demonstrated its might and majesty. There was no petty spite, no malice, no envy, no hypocrisy nor deceit in inanimate phenomena.

Reluctantly the Tec reined in his imagination and reviewed the circumstances surrounding the death of Edlin Borrowitch, an event of small importance on the cosmic stage, but of final significance to the Bizman himself. He considered the suspects.

Firstly there was Ros Kernwell, the 'favourite', so to speak. She would certainly have had the opportunity. The means she might easily have come by. The native vegetation was loaded with plant bio-chemicals which were toxic to terrestrial life forms. Simply by stewing up a handful of the local herbs with water and filtering off the fibrous matter, she could have produced a mixture of variable delay poisons such as the one that caused the death of the Bizman.

The question of motive was more problematic. If Ros Kernwell's behaviour was strictly logical, she could not have been the murderer, since her interests had not been well served by the Bizman's death. However, human beings rarely behaved logically, at least not according to a logician's concept of logic. She might be stupid, but he altogether doubted that. She might have panicked. On the face of it, that seemed more likely, especially since her disappearance now strongly suggested she was no more immune to panic than anyone else. However, in his experience, poisoning rarely resulted from panic — the preparations were too lengthy, the commission too surreptitious for it to be a panic weapon.

Secondly, there was the Bizman's wife, Adelin Borrowitch. She had opportunity in superabundance, and the means she could acquire as easily as Ros. There was no definite motive, but there were all sorts of possibilities. Even seemingly trivial problems could be magnified in the close relationships of marriage, magnified to the point where only a desperate act would offer any prospect of relief. Could the Bizman's desire for another child have been such a problem? Could Adelin have become romantically attached to the elder of her two stepsons? Or, more nebulous, but perhaps more potent, could her juvenile political beliefs have begun to reassert themselves, perhaps under the malign influence of Nadya Lasolere? There were too many possibilities.

He turned to a consideration of the Bizman's sons.

Both had ample opportunity and the same access to the means as anyone else on Dorado. Jaimi appeared to be one of the few people with a pressing, uncomplicated and obvious motive. He needed credit. Without it, he was a prisoner in his module. Denson didn't think Jaimi was the type to accept confinement philosophically. He seemed just the sort of sulky, amoral egotist who would have no qualms, filial or otherwise, about hastening the advent of his inheritance. Whether guilty or not, he should at any rate be worth a few points in Ros Kernwell's favour on the Guilt Probability Index.

The Tec had yet to meet Obert, but from the information he had gleaned, the elder Borrowitch son seemed altogether a more complex personality, and therefore less predictable, and perhaps less stable.

Expected to succeed his father as head of the Borrowitch business empire, he had latterly shown the classic sign of impiety — attraction to a diametrically opposed way of life. It was an effect which occurred in most children during puberty. In Obert it had been delayed, and might be all the more recalcitrant for that. Nevertheless, murder was hardly likely to be found among the teachings of the Brotherhood of Earth. Obert might have so misconceived his duty to the Earth Mother as to encompass the death of his father, but Denson doubted it. If he could only meet and speak with Obert, the Tec felt he would have no difficulty making up his mind on that point. To do that, however, it seemed he would have to pursue him to Joy City.

Nadya Lasolere was an entirely different proposition. Her friendship with Adelin could have given her the opportunity, and also the motive. Furthermore, the Tec thought he had detected an underlying viciousness in her temperament which could predispose her to criminality in pursuit of her ambitions

— but perhaps he was just still sore at himself for passing up the opportunity she'd offered.

What of the Bizman's professional associates? Denson was inclined to discount them, although there was definitely something out of the ordinary in Borrowitch's relationship with Cluth. It would be interesting to see if the interaction between Borrowitch and his other business contacts were similar or dissimilar to those with Textiles Marketing.

It seemed to the Tec that his next step must involve a trip to Joy City — Obert was presumably there, and Ros Kernwell might well be. It would also give him the opportunity to look up Shani Chandon of Fantasy Fabrics.

Denson got up and crossed to the window. He stared out over the metropolis, somnolent in the afternoon sun. He wondered what Seelya was doing. Suddenly he felt an overwhelming need to talk to someone quite uninvolved in the case, to forget about it for a while. He called the number the girl had given him, half expecting that there would be no answer, and was delighted when her face formed in his communications globe.

'What on Old Earth have you been up to?' she exclaimed, her eyes wide, and a flattering expression of concern on her beautiful features.

Sarn remembered that he'd taken no time to clean up after the incident on the cableway. He glanced at the monitor below the globe, which showed the image he was projecting of himself. He looked dusty and tired, and there was a bruise on his temple and a trickle of congealed blood from his forehead. The contrast with the flawless appearance of Seelya in the globe made him feel uncomfortable.

'I'm sorry,' he apologised. 'I had a bit of a bump — I'd quite forgotten it. I'll clean up and call you back, if I may.'

'I'm coming straight over!' decided the girl firmly. 'Don't go anywhere until I've made sure you're up to it.' She grinned mischievously. 'I'll give you a thorough check over.'

Her image dissolved before Denson could reply.

★ ★ ★

In the early evening, the Tec and the girl decided to go down into the city for a meal. As they headed towards Denson's favourite Phecdan restaurant, he told her that he would be out of Gold City for a few days.

'On the trail?' she smiled.

'I need to do some routine checks in Joy City,' he replied.

'Nice place for a few days,' she commented. 'Sure it isn't a holiday?'

'I wish it was,' grunted Sarn. 'I reckon I need one. I don't seem to be making any headway with this Borrowitch case.'

'Perhaps you're looking in the wrong direction,' suggested Seelya.

'You mean maybe Ros Kernwell is guilty all along?'

'Just that,' nodded the girl.

Denson sighed. 'Could be, but I don't feel it that way.'

'I know Joy City pretty well,' commented Seelya casually. 'Maybe I should come with you. I might be able to help. At least I'd give you some cover.'

Denson grinned. 'You'd just make me more conspicuous, a stunning number like you.'

'I'm serious!' protested the girl. 'After what happened to you today, I'm afraid to let you out of my sight.'

The Tec was surprised by her concern — he wasn't used to anyone worrying about what happened to him. A trip to Joy City (or anywhere) would certainly be more fun with Seelya along, but one of his few principles was never to mix detection with dalliance. It wasn't so much that he feared loss of concentration, but if the going should get rough, he'd be unable to protect himself, let alone a companion.

'I wouldn't get in the way,' promised Seelya. 'I might even be able to help. I used to work in Joy City, so I know my way around. Know quite a few useful people too — like Shani Chandon, that woman from Fantasy Fabrics.'

'Really?' remarked Denson. 'She was one of Borrowitch's associates.'

'Was she?' answered Seelya. 'There you are then, perhaps I could help.'

'I don't think I could pay you much,' ventured Denson dubiously.

'I don't want paying!' flared Seelya. 'I just want to come with you!'

'Don't be offended,' begged Denson hastily. 'It would be best for you to be registered as my assistant and accept a small fee. If anything unpleasant should happen, you'd be able to claim what protection the Guild of Tecs affords its members. All I meant was that I'm doubtful about being able to claim expenses on this job, so I couldn't promise a proper fee for assistance.'

'I've already said I don't want payment,' Seelya insisted. 'I'm not short of credit. But if you think I'd just be a nuisance, say so. I don't want to thrust myself in where I'm not wanted.' Suddenly she giggled. 'I'd rather you did the thrusting!'

Denson capitulated. What were his principles anyway, if not a rationalisation of his own feelings of inadequacy?

'Well,' he replied weakly, 'if you'd really like to come . . . '

He grinned. 'It would mean I wouldn't be so desperate to get back to Gold City if you were with me . . . '

9

Joy City

It was rather late the following day when Sarn Denson and Seelya Koto left the Tec's module and headed out on the intercity cableway towards the famed — and ill-famed — pleasure capital of Dorado. Sarn was enjoying life. It felt good to have a beautiful woman by his side in the car. The day was fine and bright, but the air was not yet too hot. Below glinted the green crystals of the Great Glass Desert, and above them hummed the wires. Denson switched the car to the fast cable and they whirred past a convoy of heavy transports.

About mid-day, the Tec picked up the slip wire for Half-way Oasis, and slid the car into a vacant berth on a parking pylon. A moving path carried him and the girl into the central complex. A vast dome sheltered the oasis from the arid air and the brilliant sun, and protected the tender terrestrial plants from the alien conditions of Dorado. Denson led the way to a table close to the pool which was the heart of the complex. An artificial breeze disturbed the birches which fringed the water and ruffled the grass, which was as green as the Great Glass Desert, but infinitely softer. Sarn and Seelya studied the menu as it flowed across the surface of the table. Denson murmured their order.

'Thank you, sir,' purred the table, and a section of its surface slid open. Their meal rose from the centre of the table and they set to.

The Tec looked around with satisfaction. If he ignored the distant arch of the dome, he could imagine himself on far-away Earth. He wondered what it was like living on Earth now. He supposed there were still wild animals there. On Dorado, practically all organisms were hostile to Mankind.

There were other tables sat at discreet distances, and he was well aware that he was the object of envious stares from other men on account of Seelya. This and the surroundings, the food and the wine, combined to create a sense of well-being which made him reluctant to resume the journey. As a result, it was late when they entered the environs of Joy City.

They were held up by long queues at the toll gates on the exit of the intercity cableway, caused by the inability of a driver to pay the charge and his subsequent attempt to crash through the barrier, which severely damaged several wires. They finally negotiated this obstacle only to be met with further delay at the entrance to Joy City cable system. Eventually, however, Denson obtained the necessary licence and the car whined into the main approach.

The towers of the city reached high into the sky, tall and slender, crowned with mushrooms and cornets, rotating disks and circling modules. Large transparent bubbles floated through the air, bursting on contact to release clouds of aphrodisiac perfumes. Lights flashed and winked, flames flared, great swathes of illumination travelled through the darkening sky, banishing incipient stars. And there was music. It came in waves through the excited air, pulsing and soaring. Magnificent chords thundered across the sky, tumultous crescendos smote the ear, to be washed away by sweet, soothing melodies and harmonies. The citizens of Joy were drenched in sound. It trickled from windows and doorways, it poured from street speakers. They were deluged with rhythm, harmony and melody. Songs, symphonies and sonatas flowed forth from music shops, folk tunes and popular ballads thrummed in the taverns, and the deep rhythms of the primeval past beat forth from cellars and street stalls.

It should, thought Denson, have been the most hideous cacophony, yet somehow it made a strange harmony, as though the air seized each shred of sound and wove it into a symphonic tapestry, music which moved and merged and multiplied through all the streets and squares of the most sensuous, sensitive and sinful city on all the worlds of Man.

As the car hummed along the main artery of Joy, it was bathed in ever-changing hues; it glowed and phosphoresced as establishments for gambling, dancing, eating, drinking, loving, hating, watching, listening and even praying, flashed their gaudy advertisement on the air above the cableway, exciting the very molecules of the atmosphere into brief flashes of life to entice the traveller to sample their wares. The music, too, bore enthralling messages, sung in siren voices, chanted in chorused chords, proclaiming and naming the virtues of vices, the places of satisfaction.

'All we need is a decent hotel,' muttered Denson.

'Follow me, sir,' hissed a voice in his ear. 'I know the very place . . . '

'Don't listen!' whined another. 'Heed *me!*'

Angrily, the Tec swatted the miniature advertising bugs and closed the car windows to exclude the electronic pests.

Seelya grinned. 'Don't hit me, but I know the very place!'

Sarn smiled. 'You're one advertisement that would lure me any time!'

The girl took control of the car and whisked it off the main cableway into the maze of narrow streets that comprised the old city. The Tec admired the skill with which she slipped from one wire to another as she criss-crossed the densely packed thoroughfares. Finally they hit a wider route, where double hawsers allowed Seelya to overtake slower traffic, weaving from wire to wire and even using empty parking bays. They emerged on to a broad boulevard which snaked along beside the wide river bisecting the city. Seelya brought the car to an abrupt halt alongside the platform of 'Earthside Hotel'.

Denson slid his card into the waiting machine, and almost instantly the car was moving again. It was automatically locked to a large module, which in turn began to move, rising easily up the hotel gantry until it reached the summit of the kilometre high pylon. As the module climbed, Seelya Koto and Sarn Denson left the car and entered the hotel capsule. From the summit of the pylon, they had a magnificent view of the city, of the Yellow River winding through it, and of the Mountains of the Boom, snow-capped and distant. The pylon moved gently in the wind.

'Don't you feel unsafe so far from the ground?' asked Denson.

The girl turned to him and wound her arms about his neck. 'No,' she said. 'Just deliciously alone.'

Denson remained grumpy.

'It must be safe,' reasoned Seelya, 'or the owner would never have got planning permission from the insurance company.'

'What makes you think the building's insured?'

'Don't be silly!' chided Seelya. 'No one would risk being sued without adequate insurance.'

★　★　★

The next day, they took the module back to ground level and set off for the centre of the city. Denson wanted to consult a local Tec agency, and Seelya thought she would spend some time sight-seeing.

Before he'd left Gold City, Denson had consulted the register at the Tec Guild Hall, and had selected the Pawl Momad agency from the list as being the most likely to suit him. They had a small office in a rigid building in Love Lane, just off Drunkard's Walk in the Babylonia precinct of the urbanopolis. Seelya dropped him there, and blew him a kiss as she scorched away in his cable car. He hoped the car was still the same shape next time he saw it.

His Tec Guild card gained Sarn immediate admittance through the security door. A tall man with a dusky countenance came forward to greet him.

'Tec Denson. It is a pleasure to meet a colleague from Gold City. I'm Pawl Momad. Come into my private office and we'll have some refreshment.'

Denson thanked him. As he followed Tec Momad into his inner sanctum, he wondered exactly what mechanism the door used to transmit information from calling cards to the Tec. When they had exchanged pleasantries and drank a slug of Draconis fine distillate, Denson outlined his needs to Momad.

'I must find Accountant Kernwell,' he concluded, 'but I don't want anyone else to know where she is, and I don't want her frightened into running again.

When you've located her, just let me know. I'm also anxious to talk to Obert Borrowitch. I don't mind if you frighten him — it might make him more talkative — just as long as he doesn't lose you. After that, I'd like any local dirt there is on members of the Borrowitch clan and on the Bizman's associates.

'You must have a big policy client to be spreading all this credit around,' Momad commented.

Sarn grimaced. 'Don't worry. You'll be paid.'

'I've got a direct line into Joy Gossip from here. I can probably get you some information fairly quickly — unless you've got other lizards to fry . . . '

'Not a clue,' sighed Denson morosely.

He sank back in his chair while Pawl Momad busied himself at a console. Almost immediately, Momad swung round and handed him a hard copy. 'There's something to be going on with.'

Denson took the thin sheet and perused it:

Jaimi Borrowitch, son of a prominent

Gold City Bizman, caused a sensation in the Ophiuchi Night Dive when he hit a losing streak at the table. In a last desperate bid to turn his luck round, the youthful gambler offered a night with beautiful Petronelle Gradski, one of Fantasy Fabrics' top models, as his stake in lieu of credit at the gaming table. This was too much for the proud Petronelle, who told Borrowitch to take his attentions elsewhere, whereupon she left Ophiuchi's, and the pair have not been seen together since.

'Anything else?' asked Sarn.

'Not yet,' replied Momad. 'One of the problems is that hardly anybody in Joy City uses their own name, or even sticks to an alias long enough to accumulate a record, so snippets have to be pieced together. Of course, it's impossible to keep secrets here, and identities can normally be unravelled, but it usually takes time. Borrowitch and Gradski are both too well known to fool Gossip Incorporated for long.'

'In that case, I might as well have a look at this girl. Have you an address for her?'

Momad played the keyboard again and a brief message glowed on the screen:

* * *

Petronelle Gradski, 63rd module, 95th pylon, Musk Way, North Quarter.

* * *

Sarn decided to hire a cable car since Seelya had his. Leaving Pawl Momad's office, he walked along the street in the direction of the nearest rental agency. It always gave him a feeling of strange unreality to proceed on foot along one of the wide and almost deserted paved ways which lay beneath the humming hawsers of the overhead system.

Above him, the wires were clogged with traffic, but here, in the nearest Joy City had to a business centre, there were few pedestrians. In some of the newer cities of Dorado, the companies had made no effort to pave the streets, but had simply burnt the vegetation below the wires to prevent it snagging the overhead cars. Here in Joy City, as in Gold City, the streets had been paved centuries ago, when wheeled vehicles were still in use. The alloyed gold was hard and incorruptible, and nowadays got little use except on the boulevards of the pleasure shops.

The scarcity of walkers made shadowing someone particularly difficult, so it was hardly surprising that Denson soon became aware that he was being followed. At the next corner he turned casually left and then ran to the next intersection and slipped round the corner. He leaned against a wall, panting.

'I'm getting old!' he thought. 'Time I did some real exercise again.'

His breathing slowed, and he listened. There was the thud of feet in the street which he had just been down, and the sound of laboured breathing.

The Tec smiled grimly. It sounded as if his follower was as much a fish out of water as he was himself when it came to tearing around without a car. He glanced up and down the street. It was deserted. Even the cables were empty and still, vibrated only occasionally by traffic passing on a distant crossway. Buildings loomed above the narrow pavement, their windows shuttered or barren.

The footfalls and the panting were closer now, and Denson's hand closed around a tiny cylinder from one of his pockets. He withdrew it and held it at the angle of the building, at about head height. The shadow blundered into his field of vision and he pressed the base of the vial. A cloud of white vapour jetted from the tube, enveloping the man's head and shoulders. He crumpled without a murmur, and the Tec caught the sagging body and eased it to the ground. The head lolled over, and then Denson could see that it was Garwen, the Tec from City Investigators. Now he knew why Garwen had tipped him off about Ros Kernwell's flight — he'd hoped Denson knew where she was, or how to find her, and would lead him to her.

Garwen must have followed him to Joy City, so would know where Denson was staying. He and Seelya had better leave there as soon as possible. Garwen groaned. He'd be coming round soon — the knock-out gas quickly wore off.

Denson left Garwen lying on the pavement and ran quickly to the next intersection. He cut across the quarter, taking rights and lefts at intervals until he was sure that Garwen was unlikely to catch up with him. He slowed to a walk. He was in a narrow, squalid street. Bits of old cable, a wrecked cable car, scraps of metal and plastic littered the ground. Blank walls stifled the alleyway, which was long and twisting. Rounding a corner, he saw a figure standing in the centre of the passage.

Denson stopped, frozen by a chill of apprehension. The man started towards him slowly. His face was in shadow, his hands hanging loosely by his side. He moved with an air of menacing purpose on silent feet.

The Tec retraced his steps to the corner and looked cautiously round, with the utter certainty that there would be a second menacing presence at his rear.

There was. His mind raced furiously. The two hit men were bigger and heavier than he was, and he had no doubt that they would be well prepared. They obviously weren't out to kill him, otherwise they'd have just shot him down. They meant to frighten him — and they were succeeding! They must reckon that being a Tec, although he'd have a hefty life policy, he was unlikely to be able to afford cover for any lesser degree of violence: it was too much an occupational hazard in his line of work.

Sarn fingered the ring on his right hand. He glanced at the two men. They were moving steadily towards him. Their gaze upon him, they nevertheless negotiated the rubble-strewn alleyway with precison. Denson considered his knock-out canister, but he couldn't believe he'd get a chance to use it. He had a small laser pistol, but he couldn't hope to drop them both, the angle between the men being almost a hundred and eighty degrees, and he was certain that if he shot one, the other wouldn't hesitate to burn him, death policy or not.

He cast about for a weapon and spied a discarded iron bar. He ⸤ stooped and grasped it. It was of good quality metal, the surface alloyed with gold to prevent corrosion. Thus armed, he turned on the thug who'd followed him and began to run towards him.

His follower stopped in his tracks and calmly drew a pistol from his pocket. He raised it and fired. Denson ducked away, knowing it was too late, but the gun was not aimed at him. He realised it was an electric discharge pistol when the bolt struck the iron bar and made his arm throb. Involuntarily, his hand unclenched and the metal cudgel dropped to the ground. His assailant resumed his slow advance. The deliberation was the most unnerving feature of the ambush. It emphasised the professionalism of the two bully-boys. They must know there was no chance of them being disturbed in this remote and deserted passage of the pleasure city.

Even disarmed, he'd have more chance against one than he would against two, so he resumed his run towards the following thug. The latter halted his advance and began to retreat with equal deliberation. This puzzled Denson, until he glanced over his shoulder and saw that the other ambusher was now running and closing the gap between them as rapidly as Denson had been closing with the first. Once again he marvelled at their precision. Whoever was employing them must have been paying handsomely to secure such efficiency.

The Tec soon realised that, whatever he did, he would encounter both assailants at the same moment, so he stopped still and waited, recovering his breath and racking his brains. His stalkers resumed their unhurried advance.

The inevitable moment arrived when they were almost within striking distance of him. He had calculated that this was the one instant at which he might get at one of them separately, and at the opportune moment Denson sprang. But the man was ready for him. He leapt back, and at the same moment his confederate jumped Denson from behind. The Tec had a confused impression of the zombie features of a close-fit face mask, and then he was on the ground with an aching arm and a contused shin, his lip bleeding and one eye closed.

As he resigned himself to the prospect of a certain beating, the faint hum of an approaching hawser kindled a small spark of hope. His attackers must have heard it too, and uncharacteristically they hesitated. Denson seized the opportunity and rolled away, at last succeeding in getting both men on the same side of him, and pulling his laser pistol from his pocket in the same movement.

The men were fast, but their carefully practised plan of action had now been interfered with, and their first instinct was for survival. They dived for cover behind a heap of mainly metal rubbish which had accumulated against one of the alley's walls, drawing their own pistols as they did so. Denson scrambled quickly behind the wrecked cable car as a laser beam seered the spot where he had just been. But the wires were throbbing now, and the thugs had no stomach for complications. They broke cover and made for the end of the alleyway.

Denson let them go, as a heavily armoured cable car hove into view.

The Tec stood up straight and made signals to it, so that it came to a grinding halt just above him. A flexible ladder snaked down and he seized it gratefully, hauling himself up with slight difficulty towards the swinging patrol car. A cheerful Claims Prevention Officer pulled him inside.

'You were lucky,' commented the CPO.

Denson agreed. When activating the alarm concealed in his ring, he'd had no real hope that an insurance company prowl car would be anywhere within the immediate area. There weren't very many of them owned by the insurance companies, and they were only likely to respond to a call from one of their own policy holders, so the chances of one being close enough to come to his assistance were slim, especially in this twilight zone of the city. Normally they prowled the rich commercial areas, where the probability of foiling a crime and thus avoiding a substantial claim was high enough to warrant the expense.

'We were taking a short cut back from our normal base to the district office, otherwise you wouldn't have stood a chance of getting us here in time.'

'Well I'm glad you came,' replied the Tec, 'otherwise I'd be a heap of jelly by now.'

The CPO grinned. 'I see. It wasn't just an assassination job then; it was a putoff.'

Denson nodded. 'Between you and me, I guessed that, and since I've only got a Death Policy, with no Grievous Bodily Harm cover, I suppose I shouldn't have activated the alarm, but I don't mind telling you I was scared. Those heavies were so professional it was unnerving. They could have beat me to within a heart-beat of my life with absolute precision. Even if the company hadn't had to pay out on the crime policy, there'd have been a hefty claim on the Health Policy, if not on the total incapacity clause. So I don't feel too bad about calling up you boys.'

'Don't feel guilty at all, pal,' answered the CPO. 'I'm glad we could help. We aren't all as mercenary as the actuarial department would like, you know.'

The driver interrupted them: 'Where were you heading when you were waylaid?'

Denson told him.

'I'll drop you at Seventh Heaven Street in the North West quarter. You can hire a car there, and it isn't far from Ecstasy Avenue. Musk Way is at the far end.'

'Thanks,' replied the Tec.

'Are you going to drop your case?' asked the CPO.

'Not likely!' answered Denson grimly. 'But I'm going to be a lot more careful in the future . . . '

10

The Girl on the Screen

Denson didn't like hired cars. It was true
they were usually newer models than his
own, more luxurious, smarter, altogether
more status enhancing, but he felt no
rapport with them. With his own car, he
could tell when something wasn't quite
right — he could often guess when a
breakdown was likely, and when he drove,
his actions were second nature to him.

In a borrowed car, he felt out of place
and apprehensive, and there was no way
of knowing if it ought to be making that
strange ticking noise, or if the squeal of
the wheels on the cable usually sounded
so high-pitched. He found the controls
were invariably slightly displaced from the
position at which his hands automatically
sought them, and the vehicle always
seemed larger than his own, so that he
was constantly assailed by the irrational

fear that he might crash broadside into a car on an adjacent wire at the slightest swing of his own.

Partly to distract himself from these discomforting thoughts, and partly to check whether any further facts about the Borrowitch case had been publicised, Denson slipped his plastic receiving licence into the video slot of the car. The Tec subscribed to two news networks, telling himself it was necessary for his work, despite the cost. Without the plastic squares, inside each of which was concealed an intricate receiving circuit compatible with a particular network's transmission code, it was impossible to receive an unscrambled broadcast from the network studios.

The screen came to life, and the newscaster was an elderly male with silver hair and a soft but insistent voice.

' . . . latest news from Trans-Dorado Broadcasting Network. So much for the planet-wide cast — now for the local events.'

The man faded from the screen, to be replaced by another, younger and brasher.

' . . . one of the most serious accidents

this year. Seventeen cars were involved. At least six people are believed to be dead and twenty injured. The northbound wire of the Gold City to Mine Deep expressway is closed to all traffic, and it will be some time before the dislodged cables are re-hung.

'After one of his family was killed by the notorious Yellow River Mobsters. Bizman Delacroix of Big Find hired a detachment of militia from the Mercenaries Company of Gold City, and in an exchange of fire today, the Mercenaries wiped out most of the Mob.

'In Golden Plain, the Safety First Insurance Company failed in its bid to bring the Golden Gang to answer charges. Several insurance agents were killed in the battle which erupted when Safety First men stormed the Gang's headquarters in Golden Plain. A spokesman for Safety First said the payout on the policy they were enforcing is now exhausted, and they had no plans for another attempt on the Gang. However, there is speculation that the dead agents themselves carried heavy indemnities which may finance a renewal of hostilities when the claims are settled.

'Miners Mutual Insurance today announced a half per cent increase in transport insurance premiums, and predicted that other companies will soon be forced to follow suit as a consequence of the increasing number of cableway accidents. Other major companies were quick to deny any planned increases, and went as far to say that poor risk assessment was to blame for Miners Mutual's problems, and that drivers would do well to consider switching insurers.

'The Borrowitch murder mystery continues to intrigue the gossip hounds in Gold City, and to worry the business community. City Investigators, who have been retained by Aurum Life, say they are following up a promising lead — which probably means they are as puzzled as the rest of us.'

Denson removed his licence, and the newscast ceased abruptly. He had reached the Ecstasy Avenue turn-off, and he slowed the car, engaged the second wheel set on the left side branch cable, and released the first set from the main wire. The branch cable took a sharp curve into the avenue. He drove rapidly to the end and turned into Musk Way.

The 95th pylon was an expensive looking chromium plated stem with clusters of gleaming modules suspended from elegant cantilevers. There was parking at the base, and Denson slid his car into a vacant bay. He took an elevator to the sixth cantilever, and walked out along the transparent walled corridor to the third module. The figure 63 glowed a delicate pink on the door.

Denson pressed his palm against the identification panel. The number faded from the door, but it remained shut.

'Who is it?' enquired a musical voice.

'I'm a Tec,' replied Denson. 'I'd like to talk to you about the death of Bizman Borrowitch.'

'Press your guild card against the door,' requested the woman.

Sarn complied and the occupant was presumably satisfied, since the door slid open.

Denson stared. Framed in the doorway was the girl who had been dancing on Jaimi Borrowitch's tape. There was no mistaking the beautiful, provocative face, and, although her body was now clothed, it was covered rather than concealed.

'Well?' prompted the dancer.

'Sorry,' mumbled the Tec. 'I thought for a moment I'd seen you somewhere before.'

Petronelle Gradski smiled archly. 'I liked your first approach better,' she commented.

Sarn pulled himself together, and mentally cursed his naïvety. It was past time that he learned to accept the unexpected without registering astonishment so openly.

'I spoke the truth,' he said at last. 'I do need to ask you some questions in connection with the murder.'

'And I think you were speaking the truth the second time too!' remarked Petronelle Gradski. 'But you don't just *think* you've seen me before, you *know* it, but for some reason you're reluctant to admit it. You're one of those unfortunate people who hate to tell an out and out lie, but can reconcile their conscience with a misrepresentation.'

Sarn Denson smiled ruefully. 'You should be the Tec, not me.'

The woman laughed. 'Come in,' she invited. 'I think I might enjoy being interrogated by you.'

Petronelle Gradski's module was decorated with swathes of material, shimmering satins, sparkling synthetics, precious plastics, ebullient brocades, colourful cottons. They hung on the walls, concealed the ceiling, covered cushions, frothed and flowed from baskets and bags. Petronelle herself wore a plastic of silvery sheen — two rectangular sheets fastened together at the shoulders with silver brooches, but nowhere else apparent to Denson. As the girl moved across the room, the Tec caught tantalising glimpses of her body, seemingly bare beneath the ankle-length coverall. Petronelle Gradski reclined on a silk-covered divan, her head resting on her elbow, one long slim leg escaping from the inadequate confines of her dress, and smiled reassuringly at the Tec.

'Model Gradski,' he began.

The girl giggled. 'If you address me so formally,' she interrupted, 'I shall be unable to stop laughing for long enough to answer your questions. Call me Petronelle if you wish to put me at my ease.'

'Very well, Petronelle,' Denson began again, only to be interrupted once more.

'I hope you will return the compliment by entrusting me with your personal name,' went on the Model.

'It's Sarn,' grunted Denson, 'as you no doubt saw from my guild card. Do all models converse in this exhaustingly polite way?'

Petronelle laughed. 'Sorry,' she said, without contrition. 'I was making fun of you. You looked so pompous.'

Denson smiled. 'Look, suppose I get down to business? You knew Jaimi Borrowitch?'

'Yes, as you know already, else you wouldn't be here.'

'You had a bust-up with him in public. Seen him since?'

Petronelle shook her head. 'He was

amusing for a while, but he was stupid about gambling. Gambling bores me, and it made a boor out of him.'

'Jaimi doesn't gamble any more,' commented the Tec.

'Really?' Petronelle arched her brows.

'He doesn't do anything much any more,' Sarn went on, 'except watch a tape of you dancing.'

Petronelle Gradski actually blushed. She bit her lip. 'I rather regret making that.'

'Why?' asked Denson, quick to press home the opening it had taken him so long to achieve. 'It showed you to good advantage.'

'It certainly seemed to make an impression on you!' retorted Gradski. 'That was obviously where you 'thought' you'd seen me before. Did Jaimi show you the whole tape?'

'No,' admitted the Tec regretfully.

'I wonder where he got it,' mused the girl.

'He said a friend sent it to him,' replied Denson.

'Acquaintance perhaps,' returned Petronelle tartly. 'I doubt whether he has any friends.'

Sarn smiled at the barbs of malice.

'Jaimi Borrowitch stood to regain financial freedom by the death of his father,' he remarked casually, and then glancing up sharply from beneath lowered brows, he continued softly: 'Would he have had the guts to bump off his old man to gain his inheritance?'

Petronelle Gradski hesitated, and there was uncertainty in her reply: 'Is that really a pertinent question? Wouldn't it be more to the point to ask if he would be likely to do it?'

'It might, but it isn't the question I would like answered,' persisted the Tec.

'I . . . I think Jaimi lacked the resolution needed for premeditated murder. Anyone might kill on the spur of the moment.'

The Tec raised his eyebrows. 'You really believe that?' he asked. 'Anyone?'

'Yes,' Petronelle coloured. 'Don't you? You're a Tec. You can't have any illusions.'

'Illusions of innocence would be bad for business, you think?' commented Denson sardonically. Abruptly he changed tack: 'You work for Fantasy Fabrics?'

'Yes,' the model answered quickly, and

167

relief was evident in her voice. 'That is to say, they frequently engage me. I'm not an employee. Like most models, I prefer to freelance. In any case, there are few fashion houses big enough to retain girls on a permanent basis.'

'Isn't it a rather insecure occupation?' asked Denson.

'Isn't yours?' retorted the girl.

The Tec smiled wryly. 'Check,' he agreed. 'How did you come to meet Jaimi?'

'I don' really remember,' replied Petronelle Gradski. She had abandoned her casually provocative pose, and now sat bolt upright on the divan, striving to keep anxiety from her voice. Denson was puzzled by her change in attitude, and continued to probe.

'That's odd — I normally remember where I first encounter people, even casual acquaintances.'

'Perhaps that's because you're a trained observer,' shrugged the girl. 'I meet so many people that I find it difficult to recall all of them, never mind the circumstances in which we met.'

168

'But J. Borrowitch wasn't just someone you met — you had an intimate relationship.'

'Not really. Not especially so.'

Sarn sighed. 'From all accounts, it sounded intimate enough to me — despite my credulity at human innocence.'

Petronelle Gradski flushed. 'I don't think I want to talk to you any more,' she said and rose lithely. Denson remained seated.

'Did you know E. Borrowitch?' he queried.

Despite her anger, the girl sank back, non-plussed by his quiet persistance and sudden change of tactic.

'Yes of course. He was closely associated with Bizwoman Chandon and often visited Fantasy Fabrics. Sometimes I was there when he came. He was always interested to meet Shani's models.'

I'll bet, thought Denson. Aloud he said: 'Perhaps Jaimi was with him at times?'

'Perhaps he was,' returned Petronelle, but without conviction.

'Maybe that's where you met him?' suggested the Tec.

Model Gradski shrugged. 'Could be. I can't see that it's important.'

'Perhaps not,' agreed Sarn Denson, 'but I'm trying to build up a background to the family — trying to get a picture of how they lived. How well did you know Edlin Borrowitch?'

'Only casually.'

'Like Jaimi?'

Petronelle Gradski jumped up again. 'You really are objectionable!' she blazed. 'Get out before I call my insurers and get them to sue you!'

'Sure,' soothed Denson, easing himself out of the chair. 'I'm on my way. It was a pleasure seeing you — again . . . '

He stopped in the corridor outside, and fished a slightly conical disc out of his pocket, pressing it against the wall. He applied his ear to the shaped nipple and concentrated. Sounds came to him faintly.

' . . . he asked a lot of questions.'

Pause.

'No, they didn't make a lot of sense. He didn't seem to have anything specific in mind, but perhaps for that very reason I found them unsettling . . . '

Another pause.

'No he didn't. He did ask about Edlin.'

Finally: 'No, of course not. I'll be in touch some time.'

Denson moved away. It had obviously been Petronelle Gradski's side of a personal communication — but to whom? Her insurer possibly — a routine report in case of consequences — but if not that, then perhaps to Jaimi? Or some other member of the clan. In which case, was Model Gradski involved in some way with the Borrowitch case?

The Tec left Musk Way and retraced his route to the Pawl Momad agency. He hung his rented car on the parking cable and went through the armoured doors into the atmosphere of security which the agency exuded. He wondered how much it would cost to maintain an office as well protected as the Pawl Momad agency.

Momad himself came forward to greet him.

'How did you get on?' the big man asked.

'Better than seemed likely at one stage,'

171

was all Denson would vouchsafe.

'I've some more news for you,' went on the agency chief. 'Arick Earthborn and Zarah Borrowitch have blown into Joy. They're staying at the Palace Pylon out on Splendour. Better yet, we've located your client.'

He paused, but Denson had no time for dramatic effects.

'Give,' he demanded.

Pawl Momad smiled. 'She's in a hive in Sekcentexo. Number 1062, Heap Five. She's either very nearly skint, or very, very anxious not to be found.'

Denson digested this information. He'd never needed to visit any of the exocities in the course of previous investigations, but he knew about them — it was part of the essential background information that any Tec might need at any time. They were areas excluded from the operations of the insurance companies, therefore nothing that happened there could be the subject of any claim under any policy. It was just about the only clause the insurance companies had in common.

From time to time an enterprising

Bizman would set out to write policies which would extend to the Heaps and their denizens, but such attempts had always failed. Only the hopelessly poor and the determinedly criminal settled in the exocities. The former could not afford insurance — the latter would exploit it ruthlessly. Without income from the exocities themselves, the insurance companies had no real incentive to provide claim prevention patrols. There was little legitimate business that could take a respectable citizen to the Heaps, and his policies gave him no protection there.

'How did you find out?' he growled.

Pawl smiled and shook his head. 'You're paying for information, not a course in methodology. Besides, today you're a client, tomorrow you may be a competitor. Our sources are our livelihood.'

Denson made no reply, and the Joy City Tec went on.

'What are you going to do? If your client has taken refuge in a no-go area, she's almost certainly guilty. The only other possibility is that she's completely

173

broke. In neither case could you be blamed for terminating your contract. It would be madness to pursue her into the Hives — especially that one. It's so old. It must be a death-trap.'

'I'm paying for your information, not your advice,' drawled Sarn.

Pawl Momad refused to take offence. Instead he looked worried.

'It's your business, of course, but I hate to think you might go charging into the Hives completely unprepared.' He sighed. 'I'm a fool for giving away information without payment, but . . . well, let's say it's for the sake of the Guild. If you're really determined to enter Sekcentexo, then go in the garb of the Brotherhood.'

'The Brotherhood of Earth?'

Momad nodded. 'Whether it's out of superstition, or because they realise that the Brotherhood is their last hope of succour in extreme necessity, most of the inhabitants of the Hives leave the Brothers alone. Not all. There are some villainous souls who'll let nothing stop them, but if you wear the robes it might increase your chance of survival from

174

zero to about nought-point-oh-five.'

'Thanks,' acknowledged Denson. 'I hate disguise, but in this case it may be prudent. What's more, the Brotherhood fascinates me. It would be interesting to know what it feels like to be togged out in their clobber. Any idea where I can get an outfit?'

'I think we might find you one,' admitted Pawl Momad reluctantly.

'I guessed you might — how else would you have got information about Ros Kernwell out of Sekcentexo? Seriously, though, I'm grateful for the tip.'

'If I need a favour, you'd better be ready,' grumbled the Joy City Tec. 'When do you want the fancy dress?'

'Tomorrow. I've had enough excitement for one day. I'll take a look at the stagestruck lovers next and leave the rough stuff to another day.'

★   ★   ★

Tec Denson had a quick meal in an off-world cafe and then threaded the cableways to Splendour Boulevard. Pylon Palace was a cluster of knobbly spires at the city end of the throughway. As he approached, the knobs were revealed as stylish modules adhering to the tapering towers of the pylon complex. Leaving the hired car hanging in the car park, he approached the information hub and asked for Zarah Borrowitch.

'What makes you think there's anyone called Zarah Borrowitch here?' asked the front man.

'You're so quick with the name, you must have heard it before, and you can't kid me you're socially acquainted with the Borrowitchs,' jeered Denson.

'Oh no?' bridled the man. 'Supposing there was such a party here — what makes you think she'd want to see you?'

'Suppose you just check she's here,' suggested the Tec, 'then we can take it from there.'

'It's a house rule that no information about guests be given out,' replied the front man stubbornly.

'Are you a betting man?' asked Sarn, adopting a more friendly tone. The front man remained suspicious and merely stared at him.

'Suppose I bet you fifty Leonardos there's no Zarah Borrowitch staying here?'

Abruptly the front man softened. 'All right, you win — or rather lose. She's here.'

Denson took out his card and pushed it into the transfer machine on the desk. He keyed in 'Fifty Leonardos' and pressed his thumb against the signature screen, and prayed he still had some credit left in his account. As soon as he got back home he would check his accounts, he promised himself, and find out whether the overdrawn accounts outbalanced the credit ones. The machine winked green, and the front man slipped his own card into the credit slot and pressed his thumb on the window. The fifty Leonardos were automatically transferred from Denson's account to the front man's.

'Now,' pursued Sarn, 'I need to talk with Zarah Borrowitch. If you send this card up, I'm certain she'll want to see me.'

He hoped he was right as he handed over the plastic calling card, with a hastily scribbled note on the back.

'Want to bet I can't get it in the slot first time?' grinned the front man wolfishly.

Denson sighed and went through the ritualised bribery a second time. The card went into the slot and was reproduced on the screen in Zarah's module. A moment later, a reply flashed on to the desk screen:

SEND TEC DENSON UP.

11

The Exocity

Arick Earthborn was tall and dark, with a languid manner, but the restless eyes of a fanatic. Zarah Borrowitch looked small beside him, and she was possessed of a rather artificial beauty, her large features emphasised by theatrically applied make-up, as though to make them visible from an immense distance.

'I apologise for intruding on your grief . . . ' Denson began.

'Never mind all that!' interrupted the actor rudely. 'Zarah outgrew any childish feelings she had about her father ages ago. It isn't as though he ever did much for her — Edlin had no use for daughters.'

'Is that so, Zarah?' enquired the Tec softly, and thought he detected a quiver of her lip before she replied harshly:

'It is as Arick says. My father wasn't interested in me or my life. We hardly ever spoke to one another.'

'Nevertheless, you will receive a share of his estate.'

'That's typical of Edlin Borrowitch,' broke in Arick Earthborn. 'Now he's no use for his wealth, someone else can have it, but when he was alive, he begrudged every fraction of a Leonardo that wasn't spent on making more.'

'He wouldn't invest in your theatrical ventures?' There was more than a hint of sarcasm in the Tec's voice. Earthborn flushed.

'You sent us a note suggesting you might be able to increase our share of Borrowitch's estate. That's all we want to hear about. If that was just a ruse to get in here, we'll send for some removers and have you thrown out.'

'I sent a note to Z. Borrowitch. You weren't included in the address,' countered Denson harshly. 'As far as I know, you've no share in the estate, and I don't aim to increase it. My business is with Zarah Borrowitch, and if you continue interrupting, I'll insist on seeing her alone or not at all.'

Arick Earthborn's face grew a darker

shade still, but a renewed outburst was forestalled by Zarah.

'I've no secrets from Arick. You said in your note that you foresaw circumstances in which my inheritance may be considerably increased. I'm anxious to hear what you have to say.'

Denson now ignored the actor, and spoke directly to Zarah: 'It has not yet been established who killed your father . . . '

'It seems there was little doubt it was that Kernwell woman,' interrupted Arick.

'Oh, but there is doubt — very serious doubt,' returned Denson blandly, 'and that is where the increase in your fortune may arise. Should the murderer be one of the beneficiaries from the death, then on his conviction — or hers — the inheritance would be redivided amongst the remaining heirs.'

'But only members of his family stand to inherit his wealth,' pointed out Arick.

'Exactly,' agreed Sarn. 'So, if it can be established that one of your brothers — or even your step-mother — was the culprit, then you stand to gain considerably.'

'What is your interest in this?' asked

181

Earthborn sharply.

'I hoped you might consider employing me to investigate the possibility,' replied the Tec ingenuously.

'Huh!' sneered Arick and turned his head back in disgust.

'Is it just a supposition,' enquired Zarah, 'or do you have any evidence?'

'Not exactly evidence,' admitted the Tec regretfully, 'but there certainly appears to be sufficient motive in the case of each of your three relatives. For instance, your brother Jaimi has lost a great deal of money from gambling, and needs a windfall if he's to re-establish himself.'

'Not just on gambling,' countered Arick Earthborn, returning to the conversation. 'Women too.'

'Ah yes,' allowed the Tec. 'I heard about Petronelle Gradski.'

'And, after her, in Gold City, he took up with some other girl — an expensive one. I wouldn't mind betting more of his money went on her than on his gambling.'

'Do you know who she was?' enquired the Tec idly.

Arick shook his head. 'We've been away,' he said.

'So, all in all, Jaimi is a good candidate for the post of murderer,' the Tec concluded.

'No, I can't believe it!' cried Zarah. 'I won't have you discuss it so ... so brutally! He's my brother. He wouldn't kill anyone, especially not father.'

'Come on, Zarah, grow up,' urged Arick. 'Jaimi has become a very nasty piece of work.'

'Of course,' murmured Denson, 'Obert was anxious for more money too — to give to the Brotherhood of Earth.'

'It's not very likely he'd murder to get it, though,' Arick had to admit.

'Oh I don't know ... ' The Tec was at his most non-committal. 'He'd become a fanatic about the Brotherhood, and fanatics will sometimes go to extraordinary lengths to further their ideals.'

'True.' Arick brooded upon this observation.

'You are a fanatic yourself,' suggested the Tec quietly.

'Oh but he's not!' contradicted Zarah

quickly. 'He's a dedicated man — dedicated to the theatre — but that's not the same as being a fanatic.'

'Then there's your step-mother,' the Tec resumed. 'She didn't need money perhaps, but there were other pressures.'

'Her tedious secret past, I suppose,' groaned Arick. 'Surely everybody knows about that anyway — and who cares?'

'Adelin Borrowitch cared, and so did the Bizman himself. Perhaps they chose to believe it was a well kept secret. Perhaps Adelin experienced a resurgence of her former ideas.'

'If you say so,' commented the actor wearily. 'If it means more money for the live theatre project, I'll believe in anything.'

'Well I won't!' snapped Zarah, in what the Tec could well imagine was a rare display of independence. 'Neither of my brothers could have murdered father, and I can't really see Adelin doing it either. She may not have loved my father deeply, but she respected him.'

'If she didn't love him, why did she marry him?' asked the Tec.

'Well, for security I suppose. He was rich enough to provide well for her.'

'In other words, she married him for his money,' sneered Arick. 'Perhaps if she didn't stop at marrying for money, she wouldn't hesitate to kill for it. Maybe she got tired of keeping her side of the bargain.'

'Perhaps the Bizman demanded more of her,' suggested Denson softly. 'A child perhaps.'

'Do you think so?' asked Zarah with interest. 'How extraordinary . . . '

'Why should it be so extraordinary?'

'It just is — that is, the idea had never occurred to me before, so it just seemed strange.'

'There is also yourself, of course,' Sarn went on in his deceptively mild manner. 'You and Actor Earthborn are both anxious to gain funds to further your schemes. It might be asked how far you would go to raise it.'

'Now see here!' began Arick quickly, but once again Zarah Borrowitch interrupted him, and her voice was steely:

'If you think I'd pay you just so that

you could go round asking that question, then you've made a mistake. I think it would be best if you left now.'

'As you wish,' agreed the Tec amiably.

Arick Earthborn could not resist pursuing the chance of a greater fortune, despite his anger: 'Don't think that because we won't employ you to investigate the Bizman's family we wouldn't be, ah, suitably grateful if you discovered something to our advantage. When I say advantage, I really mean everyone's advantage. We're not interested in money for ourselves, but to finance a revival of true theatre — the live theatre.'

'I'll remember that,' promised Denson.

★   ★   ★

As he descended from the module via the lift, the Tec thought about the interview. He'd really learnt very little. He now had a picture of Zarah Borrowitch and Arick Earthborn to add to his portraits of the Borrowitch circle. He judged Earthborn to be quite single-minded and unscrupulous enough to commit murder if it appeared in his own interest to do so, but Zarah struck him differently, and not simply because the dead man had been her father. Beneath her obvious devotion to her lover and to the theatre, but not submerged by these, was a tough strand of conventional morality.

The one other scrap of information he'd gleaned confirmed Jaimi's predeliction for an expensive way of life, but really did nothing to further any suspicions of the younger Borrowitch son.

For a brief moment, the Tec envied the policemen of other worlds, with their disciplined organisations, and their battery of scientific and legal aids. He had only his wits. He must poke away patiently, but relentlessly, at the people involved, until the truth unfolded itself before him. He couldn't even summon people for interrogation. He must trick, cajole or frighten them into talking to him. The moment passed, as it always did.

To be honest with himself, he knew he enjoyed his existing mode of life, although he was clear-sighted enough to realise that this was probably because he was used to it. He didn't really know what being an official policeman would be like, so he had no true basis for comparison.

Denson looked at his watch, and was surprised to find it was only mid-day. It had been a heavy morning, and it felt like more than a week since he'd parted company with Seelya.

He retrieved his car and drove back towards the centre of the city. He stopped at a cableway café for a snack. He wondered what he ought to do next, or rather he tried to convince himself that there was an alternative course of action to entering the exocity. Reluctantly, he conceded defeat. He owed it to his client to speak to her again, and besides, there seemed no other line to follow. He might just as well get it over with as postpone it until tomorrow.

★ ★ ★

Pawl Momad was reluctant to give Sarn the robes of the Brotherhood, but complied. He surveyed the result.

'You'll do,' he decided, 'providing you keep your face hidden. There's nothing saintly about your ugly faceplate!'

Sarn squirmed inside the robes.

'I hope this disguise works,' he grumbled. 'If I need to take rapid evasive action, I might as well give up. I feel like a cat in a trap.'

Momad smiled a little crookedly. 'I don't know why I should be so concerned about seeing a competitor head for certain elimination — it can only increase my business.'

'Thanks for the encouragement,' growled Denson.

'Fortunately it's not too far to the hives from here. You obviously can't go there in a hired car — that would be uncharacteristic of the Brothers, but there's a public cable car route in the next street which terminates at the boundary of the city and the exocity.'

★   ★   ★

As he sat brooding within the voluminous cowl in the crowded car, the Tec endured

189

the covert observation of his fellow passengers stoically. He found it less easy to endure the afternoon heat which the heavy robes soaked up.

By the time the car reached the boundary terminus, he was the only remaining passenger. He stepped out, and descended the rickety staircase to ground level. Ahead of him stretched a waste of rubble, rubbish and refuse — a No Man's Land between the city and its feared and unwanted offspring.

There was a rough track leading from the terminus steps out across the wasteland. He picked his way along it, taking care to avoid the prickly weeds which threatened to overrun the path. As the fierce heat of Aurum beat down upon the parched wilderness across which he moved so slowly, Sarn Denson felt lonely and exposed. He sweated in the heat, and he suspected that the sweat of fear was mingling with the perspiration trickling down his back. The wooden clogs were clumsy on feet unused to them, and the hem of his robe was soon patched with evil-looking burrs.

It was with double relief — to be out of the sun, and to gain some cover — that he reached the shadows of the further side; shadows which were cast by the rearing structures of the hives. No sooner was he amongst them, however, than he was assailed by a new fear — that they would topple on him and crush him. He knew it was an irrational fear. These buildings had stood for centuries. Those that were going to collapse tumbled quickly, and there had been no new building in Sekcentexo for many years. It was the knowledge that nothing here (including himself) was insured against disaster that made him feel so insecure.

He stumbled along the base of a building until he came to a narrow fissure, an alleyway which led into the complex of the hive. Like the wilderness, it was strewn with rubbish, and the air smelt rank and rotten. With an effort, he tried to adjust his frame of mind to that of a Brother entering an area of depravity and suffering to bring counsel and comfort. There was no help to be gained from creeping along the walls. He must step out as boldly as his clogs permitted.

There seemed to be no windows, but he soon came to an arched opening, through which he could glimpse an open, but rubble-filled courtyard, on to which gazed blank and unglazed openings. He saw no people, and the silence was uncanny. He realised how accustomed he was to the whirr and hum of the cableways, which were entirely absent from the exocity.

Presently the alleyway ran out into a broader thoroughfare, and here at last he saw the inhabitants of the sinister sprawl. They moved circumspectly, keeping their distance from one another as if afraid of some contagious disease — and well they might. Denson shuddered. His health insurance would not cover any illness contracted here in the Heaps, nor any injury which might befall him.

He peered up at the towering buildings. Here and there walls bulged outwards, and in some places there were signs of collapse, mainly in the upper storeys, but further down the street a whole building had fallen, leaving a great mound of rubble spilled into the roadway. The contracting companies who had erected the tenements of the exocity, unhindered by the requirements of insurance corporations, had not troubled themselves about the safety of their structures. Those who would buy the miserable flats were lucky to get anything at prices they could afford — that was the attitude of the builders. In the circumstances, it was remarkable that anything still stood.

The street was unpaved and uneven. As in the wilderness, weeds constituted an additional hazard. The roads were unmarked and unsigned, but Denson had committed to memory a map of the route to Ros Kernwell's bolt-hole. He hoped Momad's agent's instructions were accurate.

As he made his way, a passer-by or two muttered an almost inaudible 'May the Earth Mother Bless You,' or the more simple 'Gaia Bless You,' and the Tec felt a pang of unreasonable guilt that he should be the recipient of these undeserved blessings.

Sarn had begun to get used to his habit, and to the new and unfamiliar environment, so he noticed when the street suddenly emptied, and instinct told him to take cover within a ruined arch. Peering out, he saw the reason for the exodus. A group of about a dozen men were coming down the centre of the roadway. They moved more confidently than the lone pedestrians who had now vanished, but nevertheless they kept a wary look out in all directions.

Denson could see that they carried weapons, sinister black guns, and some had grenades slung from their belts. He watched and waited. Of a sudden, a man came out of an alleyway into the street. Almost immediately he spied the gang, but it was too late. Already they had swung into action. While three of them kept watch over the main thoroughfare, the rest of the pack silently pursued the man into the alley. After a short while they re-emerged, carrying a few odds and ends, which they shared with their comrades.

Whether the fugitive had been murdered or merely robbed, the Tec did not know, but he determined to avoid any such marauders, whom he felt sure would have no respect for the robes he wore.

A new development took his attention. From the other direction, another group of men had emerged on to the street. They too were armed and alert, and they seemed to have some sort of uniform. At least, they were all dressed very much alike. As they spotted the first gang, they moved forward rapidly.

Their quarry at first hesitated between flight and attack, but then urged on by their apparent leader, they moved forward to engage the newcomers. Grenades hurtled through the air, their blast flinging bodies willy-nilly amongst the rubble. Beams and bullets from a variety of firearms charred and splintered the area. Screams and shouts of triumph echoed amongst the ruins.

Abruptly, the fight came to an end. A fleeing brigand was shot down, and nothing remained of the gang but a scattering of bodies. The surviving members of the second squad systematically stripped the bodies of their enemies. Some things they kept for themselves, but most they piled in a clearing in the centre of the thoroughfare. Then the leader produced a megaphone, through which he began to speak:

'This is Xed, elected leader of Sekcentexo Vigilantes. The Death-Hawks have been exterminated. So shall we deal with all those who prey on the poor. Their ill-gotten loot is here in the street. Take of it what you will.'

The band reformed and picked its way down the street, still on the alert. As soon as they had vanished, the braver amongst the inhabitants of the hives began to emerge, to scramble amongst the pathetically small heap of treasures in the dust. Soon nothing remained. The bodies were left where they were, but already the scavenging cats were prowling from their lairs and sniffing around them. Soon there would be little left but bones, Denson had no doubt.

Who were the Sekcentexo Vigilantes, he wondered? They couldn't be a professional peace-keeping organisation or security force, not here in the Heaps. Who would pay them? In Gold City itself there were few areas where the citizens were rich enough to employ street and precinct guardians. Had they not left most of the loot to be taken by others, the Tec would have dismissed them as a rival gang, exterminating their competitors. Their leader had claimed to be elected — that was a guild process. Could these men be some sort of guild? Certainly not one of which Denson had ever heard.

He gave up the puzzle and resumed his cautious progress through the exocity. He was relieved that there were no further incidents. The vigilante raid seemed to have left a sort of calm in its wake, and Denson even saw one or two people speak to each other.

Eventually, he came to the building in which Ros Kernwell was said to be hiding. It was a grim, square block. He entered the courtyard through an archway. Several of the ground floor rooms had 'For Sale' notices scrawled on their walls. He could see only one window that was still glazed. The rest were barred or covered with sacking. At least it was cool in the well of the building.

The Tec cautiously approached a stairway in the far corner of the building, and began to climb through the evil-smelling dark. He counted the landings. At any rate, Ros Kernwell had been able to afford a room nearer the top, safer than those on the lower floors.

He reached the corridor he sought, and counted the doors — or, in some cases, the openings. When he reached the room where he expected to find his client, he was relieved to see that it was blocked by a stout metal door.

He knocked gently, but no answer came.

12

Fraud

The Tec knocked on the door again, and this time he heard the voice of Ros Kernwell: 'Who is it?'

'It's Tec Denson,' he answered.

A hole appeared in the door at eye level, and then he heard the sound of bolts and bars moving. He was pulled inside and the door was re-fastened behind him. Then the woman clung to him, sobbing for what seemed like an age. Finally, she pulled herself together and dried her face with a dirty rag.

Sarn looked around. Some effort had been made to tidy up and clean away the mess of the previous occupation, but it was a dim and dingy hole nevertheless.

'What on Dorado made you come here?!' exploded the Tec. 'And where's Obert Borrowitch? Isn't he with you?'

199

'I didn't know what else to do,' explained Ros tearfully. 'Besides, I never realised it would be quite as bad as this. I knew I couldn't afford to live for long in Joy City on what I've saved. And why should Obert be here . . . ?'

'You should have come to me!' Denson cut in savagely.

'What for?' asked the girl with a return of her former spirit. 'You're not my banker, and credit was what I needed.'

'You need help!' exploded Sarn. 'Help to clear your name — that's what Tecs are for.'

'I can't pay you,' answered the woman dejectedly. 'You're wasting your time.'

'The insurance will pay in the end,' growled the Tec. 'I can wait.'

'Just supposing you did clear me,' Ros Kernwell persevered, 'before I was formally accused. Then there'd be no claim under the policy. The bill would come to me, and I've no credit left. I can't even pay you what I already owe, let alone any further expense.'

Sarn scowled and pushed back his cowl impatiently. 'Never mind about that. The important thing is to get you somewhere safe, or at any rate somewhere you'll be entitled to claim under your policies if anything does happen.'

'I've told you, I've no more credit,' sighed the girl wearily.

Denson reached into the depths of his robe and found the hidden pouch that all the Brothers carried. From it he produced a plastic disk.

'Take this,' he ordered. 'It's an anonymous account. It won't connect you with me, or give away your identity. Use it to find somewhere secluded but safe back in the City.'

'But I can't do that!' objected the girl.

'You must,' insisted the Tec. 'If you're killed here — which you certainly will be if you stay here — then there'll be no claim under your death policy, and no credit to meet your debts. All I'm doing is protecting the investment of time and effort I've already made on this case, mainly by making sure you stay alive long enough to pay the bill.'

The woman stared at him incredulously, and then suddenly she smiled. 'For a moment I almost believed that hard-boiled act. If it were true, you'd make an appalling investment agent. But I'll accept your offer.' She shuddered. 'I couldn't bear to refuse the opportunity of escaping from this hell. And thanks.'

'Never mind that, we've still got to get out alive,' warned Sarn. 'And we must go straight away, before it gets dark. This place is bad enough in the daylight, and I dread to think what it must be like after sundown.'

* * *

The journey back was a nightmare. Denson's disguise undoubtedly saved them from casual muggers, but they were in constant fear of the gangs which roamed through the twilight, and at the slightest alarm, they hid and held their breath. At last, however, they reached No Man's Land. They stared out across the empty prospect. Aurum was sinking towards the horizon, and Ros shivered. As they watched, a shadow detached itself from the wall close by and ran swiftly across the intervening space to disappear again on the city side.

'No doubt he seeks the richer pickings of Joy City,' muttered the Tec.

'Or perhaps he just goes to seek the illusion of security that the city offers, for a few hours,' suggested the girl.

Denson looked at her sourly, then scanned the area around them.

'The sooner we go, the better,' he said. 'This place will be swarming with cats when the sun goes down, and I've no wish to be eaten alive.'

They began the lonely walk across the wasteland, apprehensive that at any moment a beam or a bullet might strike them from the darkening ruins they were leaving behind. But they were lucky, or perhaps Denson's robes gave them final protection, and they reached the terminus without mishap.

'I never thought I'd be so glad to see a cable,' commented Ros Kernwell lightly, but beneath the banter Sarn detected the fear of someone who had lived beyond the pale of civilisation, and had counted herself lost for ever.

To distract her attention, the Tec began to question her again about the circumstances surrounding the death of the Bizman.

'I imagine the pictures in the bank were protected by the usual thumb-print locks?'

The girl nodded. 'Only Edlin and myself had access to them.'

'So if *you* didn't switch the pictures — and that's the theory I have to accept if I hope to get paid — then only the Bizman could have done it.'

'That's right,' agreed Ros Kernwell.

'Why should he do that?'

'I can only think of one reason. He was very heavily committed to this Capella-Arcturus-Fomalhaut export project. There were times when I wondered where he was getting all the credit from, but it didn't do for Edlin's employees to enquire too closely into areas outside their own direct competence. It made him huffy. I can only imagine that he was juggling his picture investment — switching genuine pictures from one bank to another to raise credit, and covering up the switches with fakes. It would be a risky business, because, although he could fool his own auditors, like me, by transferring pictures whenever he knew I would be doing a routine audit, he might easily have been discovered by a spot check bank audit.'

'It would surely be very difficult to replace a picture without the bank realising it,' objected Denson sceptically.

'Somebody did it,' reasoned Ros, 'and who better to do it than Edlin? It would have to be done when pictures were being added to or removed from the collection in genuine transactions. Then a fake could be taken in, concealed behind a genuine picture. Having removed the picture he was replacing by that fake, he would smuggle out the original hidden behind another genuine painting that the bank knew he was taking. A cursory inspection of the collection before he left would reveal no blank spaces. They don't make a minute inspection every time they make a withdrawal, naturally, although they do make a thorough audit of any paintings going in, to make sure it is genuine and therefore acceptable currency.'

The Tec thought this over. It was complicated, but it would certainly account for the presence of faked pictures in the collection. It didn't take him any closer to the identity of the Bizman's murderer, however.

'Suppose somebody had found out what Edlin was doing?' he asked. 'Can you imagine any motive that would provide to murder the Bizman?'

'Not really,' replied Ros Kernwell, 'but . . . suppose he had a confederate — yes, I think he must have done — to help him manage the other accounts. Then his partner in the deception might have double-crossed him, perhaps diverted some of the genuine pictures to accounts of his own, and Edlin found out about that . . . '

'Yes,' mused the Tec. 'That's not impossible. I wonder who might have been involved in Edlin's shady activities. Accountant Cluth seems the most likely candidate. He was very thick with Edlin — much more so than you would expect for an Accountant and a Bizman. I think it's time I paid Accountant Cluth another visit.'

★ ★ ★

By the time he'd found Ros Kernwell a suitable place to stay, where she'd be inconspicuous and wouldn't exhaust the credit in his anonymous account before he'd made some progress on the case, and returned his robes to Pawl Momad, Denson realised the day had really gone at last, and he returned to the Earthside Hotel with a feeling of relief, utterly drained by the events and strain of the day.

Seelya was in high spirits, and the Tec soon recovered from his fatigue as she plied him with drinks, subtly laced with stimulants, and ordered them both an appetising meal from the table. As they ate, her face became more serious.

'Now, I want you to tell me everything that happened today. When you came in, you looked as if you'd travelled from Tau Ceti to Sigma Draconis on a standing-room-only all-stars-stopper.'

Denson outlined the events of the day, and Seelya listened with an intentness which he found gratifying.

At the end of his recital, she said, 'No wonder you look washed out.'

'What sort of day did you have?' he asked.

'Oh, nothing exciting. Mostly window shopping.'

'That's something I never could understand. I'd rather not look at things I can't afford.' He leaned back in his chair and stretched. 'By the way, I think we'd better move from here. Garwen obviously knows where we're staying. That must be how he picked me up this morning. Any ideas for a more secluded hideaway, preferably closer to the ground?'

'Plenty,' grinned Seelya. 'There are a number of honeymoon hotels in Joy City that cater for couples who just want to be undisturbed.'

'Speaking of which, it's been a long day. Let's go to bed.'

'Of course, you must be tired,' agreed Seelya with concern in her voice.

Denson grinned. 'Being tired can wait. Sleep wasn't really what I had in mind.'

★ ★ ★

Next morning, the Tec called Textiles Marketing Incorporated in Startown and asked to speak to Accountant Cluth. He was surprised to learn that Cluth was away on a visit to Joy City — although he realised he shouldn't have been surprised. Joy City was full of fashion houses whose business was inextricably bound up with that of the textile corporations.

'Do you know where he's staying?' he queried.

'We don't give out information without clearance,' replied the automatic answering machine.

'Then get clearance from Bizman Meeran, you stupid machine!' ordered the Tec irritably.

There was a pause.

'I am authorised to inform you that Accountant Cluth is staying at Cableway Inn, Joy City.'

'Thanks,' replied Denson, the meaningless courtesy coming automatically, although he knew it was only a black box at the other end.

209

'Thank you for calling,' answered the inanimate receptionist.

Sarn glanced at the clock. They hadn't got up very early, he realised ruefully. He'd take a chance that Cluth had slept in too, and call in at the Cableway Inn. Seelya, meanwhile, had been checking hotels, and had come up with one called Lovers' Lie-Inn.

'It sounds a bit crude,' doubted Denson.

'It'll be ideal,' decided Seelya. 'No one will think of looking for you there — for one thing, it isn't pricey enough for someone working on an expense account.'

'The way this case is going, that's good news.'

★ ★ ★

The front man at Cableway Inn proved no more resistant to gambling than his opposite number at Pylon Palace, and the Tec soon learned that Cluth had been up and out early, but that he'd left word that he'd be back about eleven to meet a colleague, and that should the latter arrive first, he was to be shown up to Cluth's module.

'Well here I am,' bluffed Denson. 'Show me the way.'

'How do I know you're the guy Cluth was expecting?'

'Didn't he tell you how to recognise me?' asked the Tec.

'No,' admitted the front man. 'He simply said you — he — the visitor, that is — would be coming in from Gold City.'

Denson slipped a card out of his pocket, and exhibited it to the man, holding his thumb over the prefix 'Tec'.

'There you are. My address in Gold City. Satisfied? I'm sure Accountant Cluth would tip you well for being so careful, but since he isn't here, I'll do it on his behalf.'

This appeared to resolve the man's remaining doubts, and he called the module down. Denson got in and was whisked aloft once more. He looked around him. It was a fairly standard module for a medium rank expense account. He stuck his licence card into the viewer and settled back to watch the news while he waited.

211

After a while he felt the imperceptible downward motion of the module as it descended to pick up Cluth. He withdrew his card, and the news clicked off. He swung round to face the door. If they ever manage to eliminate that faint sensation of motion, the illusion that you were permanently on the ground would be complete, he reflected, as the door slid aside and Cluth stepped in from the hotel lobby. The door shut behind him, and again there came the almost undetectable judder.

'What the devil are *you* doing here?' exclaimed the Accountant angrily.

'Waiting for you,' replied the Tec equably. 'At least, that is what I was doing. Now I've stopped waiting for you and I'm talking to you.'

'Well you can stop talking and get out!' ordered Cluth irritably. 'I've no time to swap badinage with two-a-Leonardo Tecs.'

'Even Tecs who know about crooked credit schemes . . . ?'

The Accountant's floppy disk file slipped from his suddenly nerveless fingers, and the man sank into a chair. The Tec's blind shot had hit home. Mentally, Denson chalked up a mark to Ros Kernwell.

'Ruined,' whispered the collapsed accountant.

'Aw, come on. Don't be so melodramatic,' urged the Tec. 'I'm not interested in any of that, unless I need to be, and if you talk nicely to me, then I don't see why I should. I'm looking into Borrowitch's murder, and maybe this fraud business is connected, and maybe it isn't. That's what I want to find out.'

Absently, Cluth scooped up the disk file and set it on the table.

'I'd like to help you,' he said, 'but I can't tell you anything except that I'm sure the fraud isn't related to your investigation.'

'Let me be the judge of that,' Denson told him. 'I just want to know the details. I'd like to know who was involved, how it worked, and how much credit was at stake.'

'Only the Bizman and myself were in on the scheme, that I swear to you,' replied Cluth. 'I can't tell you any more — it would be breaking Guild rules and violating fundamental bizethics.'

Sarn pressed him hard, but Cluth had recovered from his initial shock, and back in command he proved a resolute no-man.

Eventually the Tec left, cursing himself for having lost the initiative Ros Kernwell's guess had given him. Feeling deflated, he decided to seek solace in Seelya's company.

The Lovers' Lie-Inn was a clump of stubby pylons well separated from each other amongst dense and prickly shrubbery. Seelya had given him a copy of the reservation slip before he had left their other module, and he was soon in the new one, but was disappointed to find that Seelya had not yet arrived. He wandered about the module, bounced on the bed, and flicked the windows to transparent, giving himself a magnificent view of three other modules, all with their windows opaqued. He blanked his own again, and reflected that the place really must be cheap. The pylons might well be separated, but they obviously loaded them pretty heavily.

He dropped his call-card in the receiver and tapped out the number of his office answering service. There was the usual crop of bill reminders, and seductively spoken advertisements, but amongst the chaff was a message from Accountant Cluth.

'Hi Tec Denson,' it began formally. 'I've been thinking things over. Perhaps there is more that I can tell you. However, my schedule is pretty tight at the moment, largely because of Borrowitch's death. This afternoon I have to visit one of the factories set up for the Capella-Arcturus-Fomalhaut project. If you can meet me there, I believe I could spare you a short interview. The plant is located in the south sector of Gold City, on the Gold City to Ghost City express cableway. Fourteen Hours would be a convenient time for me.'

Denson experienced a moment of elation. Perhaps he hadn't muffed his chance with Cluth after all. The Accountant must have changed his mind as soon

215

as he'd left. He checked the time of the call and found it so. Perhaps it was the parting shot that had caused the change of heart. As they had talked, Denson had suddenly realised that the face he'd glimpsed and half recognised in the gambling house on Lucky Strike Boulevard had been that of Cluth.

'A dangerous occupation for an accountant — gambling,' he'd said.

'What do you mean?' Cluth had blustered, but there had been fear in his eyes.

'I've seen you in the dens along Lucky Strike,' Denson had said quietly.

'So what?' Cluth had shrugged. 'There's no harm in gambling as long as it's kept separate from work.'

The Tec had left it at that, but now it seemed beyond doubt that the matter had worked on Cluth — hence the summons.

There was still no sign of Seelya. Denson ordered a meal from the table, and having eaten, set off across the city to the shuttle port for an afternoon flight to Gold City. He disliked flying, but there wasn't time to drive back for Fourteen

Hours. The air trip, compared with the surface journey, was very short.

The shuttle hadn't time to reach its normal cruising altitude before it was sliding gently down through the turbulent atmosphere towards Gold City . . .

13

Assassin

The ghost city expressway was slung high across a shadowed valley through which meandered a sluggish river. Denson could see the glint of metal installations on the valley floor. He exchanged wires rapidly several times to bring his car into the slow lane, and slid off the expressway on to the slip cable, which swooped down into the vale.

The prickly vegetation of Dorado stained the valley sides red and yellow, and was already encroaching on the area that had been cleared by fire. As he neared the chemical complex, Denson could see half a dozen spherical reaction vessels towering over a mass of pipes and other apparatus. It looked brave and yet slightly sinister in the alien landscape, where the blackened soil awaited the return of the native scarlet and gold.

218

He parked his car on a cable spur in front of the entrance to the plant, and approached the reception screen. He activated it and waited. It replied almost immediately:

'Accountant Cluth is working in the Administrative block. The guide will take you there.'

From the tube next to the screen issued a sphere identical in appearance to the one he'd seen at Textiles Marketing Limited in Startown. Denson followed it to the gate, which rose to let him through, and closed with such terrifying rapidity behind him that he felt the wind of its descent. He looked back at the steel-framed mesh. An instant sooner and it would have sliced him in half, he thought.

A raised walkway led above the blackened earth to a four storey building whose windows were gold tinted against the sun. The sphere led him round the side of the building to a door, which opened just as he reached it. Accountant Cluth stepped out.

'Ah, I'm glad you've come,' he said, and there was such genuine relief in his voice that the Tec was puzzled.

'I'm just about to have a look at number five reactor. Perhaps you'd care to come in with me, and we'll talk as we go.'

As they walked through the complex, Denson sniffed the air, which was full of the scent of coal chemicals, tar and naphtha. The plant seemed deserted. Even when it was operational, it probably employed few men. It would be largely automated. Those who did work here would have very routine and largely actionless jobs — watching dials and chart recorders, staring at unlit neons waiting for the warning glow that would probably never come, listening for the alarm that would almost certainly not ring, neither today, nor tomorrow; never.

Denson sometimes wondered why he'd become a Tec, but he certainly knew why he had never become a production worker. He paled at the thought of the boredom of the shift routine. There was no place in that for creative thought, for problem solving, for decision making. Minding machines that solved their own problems before you even knew about them must be the ultimate in soul destruction. Why did men do it? For the sake of a company salary, company insurance and a company pension — the sort of semi-security that a welfare world would provide for all its citizens by inflicting crippling taxes.

Cluth seemed eager to talk, and described in great detail — unnecessary detail, Denson thought — just how he and the Bizman had juggled pictures between various accounts. Abruptly he broke off, and pointed to the huge reactor vessel which now curved above them.

'That's number one reactor. It's due to go on-stream in about half an hour with a test mix for synthetic fibre production.' He sighed and drew a laser pistol from his pocket. He pointed it at the Tec.

'Unfortunately the test will not be a success. The mix will have been contaminated. Inextricably meshed with the plastic matrix will be the millions of molecules which at present comprise your body, but which will soon be homogenised with the feedstock.'

He pointed towards an open inspection port. 'In there.'

Denson attempted to think rapidly, but the only thoughts that came were how stupid and how negligent he'd been to let Cluth lull him into thinking he was on top, and how nice it would be to be somewhere else, like in Joy City with Seelya.

'Come on,' urged Cluth. 'Or I'll shoot you and stuff your body through the port!'

Reluctantly Sarn complied. He found himself clinging precariously to the edge of the opening, about a quarter of the way up the curve of the vessel. Ruthlessly Cluth hammered Denson's hands with the butt of the pistol, and, with a yelp of pain, the Tec let go of the rim and slithered down into the bottom of the reactor. He heard the port cover slide home, and the fastenings click into place.

It was pitch dark inside the reactor, and very quiet. His heart-beat sounded unnaturally loud and his breath rasped in his throat. At last, however, the chaos in his mind resolved itself, and he found himself thinking with icy precision.

Desperately he recalled the glimpse he'd had of the interior of the vessel before he had been forced inside. He'd seen precious little, his eyes unaccustomed to the gloom within, unlit but for the very portal which was his point of ingress. He felt sure, however, that he had seen some mechanism, pivoted at the lowest point of the vessel, and having long arms curving up towards the sides — a device for stirring the mixture perhaps. He moved a little and located the short column he'd expected. He traced it out with his hand and found one of the arms. It felt a sturdy structure and was covered in small paddles which no doubt would produce additional mixing, but now provided him with foot and hand holds.

Denson swung the arm until it pointed in what he thought was the direction of the inspection port. Then he began to climb. After a while, he felt the wall up which the arm was curving, seeking some sign of the port. When the wall had become almost vertical, he knew he was much too high, and that either he had not got the arm at the right part of the vessel's circumference, or the port fitted so exactly that its position could not be felt.

He thrust hard against the wall and swung the arm half a metre to his left, then he worked down the curved surface, feeling for the elusive opening. Nothing. He swung the arm a metre to his right, and worked his way up again. At exactly the expected height, he found a slight recess in the smooth wall of the vessel; a precaution against the port protruding even a fraction of a millimetre into the path of the stirring arm.

Denson glanced at the luminous figures on his watch. He'd used half the available time locating the entrance. He felt in his pocket for his laser pistol, and after taking it out, he adjusted the beam width to what he judged to be five millimetres. Then he estimated the centre of the hatch by touch and began to burn a hole through it. After what seemed like an age, a narrow shaft of daylight pierced the pitch black of the vessel's interior. Sarn squinted through the puncture. His field of vision was severely limited, but it was enough to reveal that he was in luck.

Cluth had remained to observe the start-up of the reactor. He was standing almost in line with the port, staring up at the point at which Denson remembered there had been an indicator panel. He had obviously not noticed the sudden emergence of the laser beam.

Denson felt around in another pocket and found a tiny tube. He squinted through the hole at Cluth once more, estimating the angle and distance at which he stood. Holding the tube close to the hole to enable him to read the markings on it, he adjusted a pinhead marker against the gradations on the barrel. He then held the tube against the hole and twisted the end, so that a wire began to extend through the hole and across the intervening space between him and Cluth.

At the end of the wire was a minute bead, and it hovered uncertainly as the wire reached its maximum extension, and as the infrared detector inside the bead sought its target. The Tec prayed he'd got it close enough, and his prayer was answered. Sensing the body heat of Cluth as it floated towards him, the bead trailed the wire behind it like a thread of gossamer. So small was the bead and so slender the thread that it was virtually invisible, and to the reactor-fixated Cluth, they might well have been so — until the wire touched the skin of his neck.

The instant the wire made contact, it activated the metal muscles within the protective sheath. The wire curled around Cluth's neck. An additional length spewed from the tube, and the wire slithered further round to form an extra turn about the man's neck. Cluth screamed and his hands clutched frantically at the snare. Denson, peering through the hole, saw that his quarry was hooked. He pressed his lips against the opening and called to Cluth:

'Come towards the port, or I'll tighten the wire.'

The Accountant lurched forward until he was close to the hatch.

'Now undo it,' ordered the Tec, his voice calm and incisive despite the fear rising within him as the glowing figures of his watch flickered by, counting out the seconds until the plant would be switched on.

Cluth's trembling fingers seemed agonisingly inept as he tried to operate the safety catches which secured the port. Denson dared not to urge him on lest he incited the Accountant to deliberately delay, nor did he dare to tighten the wire as an additional spur, just in case the Accountant should go completely to pieces.

A faint hiss came to Sarn's ears. The reactor was beginning to fill. At that instant, the plate came loose, and the Tec scrambled through like a scalded cat. Cluth sank to the ground, sobbing. Denson thumb-nailed an indentation on the side of the tube, and the wire leash released the Accountant. The Tec felt himself trembling with reaction.

Suddenly an alarm bell rang, and a red light began to wink on the control board. A green bulb burned into life, and the alarm was muted, while the red ceased to wink but burned a steady ruby.

Cluth staggered to his feet. 'I must go and organise a repair,' he croaked.

'Lead on,' invited Denson. 'Then we'll talk.'

They returned to the Management block, and the Accountant dispatched a robot engineer with a new cover plate for the reactor port. Then he collapsed into a chair and sunk his head in his hands.

'Now,' said the Tec. 'Why try and kill me?'

'You knew, or you guessed,' groaned Cluth. 'I did divert some of the Bizman's pictures into an account of my own. I was desperate for credit to cover losses in the gambling halls. I broke the first rule of the Guild: an Accountant should never gamble. Then Borrowitch told me he was expecting a bank audit for the Export Account — we'd bought a lot of research into new products from the Newton Research Foundation. The credit involved was enormous and their Accountants were anxious. There had been an initial audit for which Borrowitch and I had switched pictures from the Textiles Account. I didn't expect them to call for a second one so soon.'

'So you panicked. You knew an audit would expose your double-cross and ruin you. But if the Bizman was dead, your fiddle wouldn't matter — all that would matter would be the massive fraud perpetrated on the Bizman's accounts. If the Bizman were blamed, that would be of no consequence to you, and the only person apart from him likely to be accused would be Ros Kernwell, since she had access to the accounts. So you killed the Bizman.'

'No I didn't,' protested Cluth. 'I admit I was relieved at his death, but I didn't do it.'

'And I suppose you didn't sabotage my car while I was in Startown, nor try to bushwhack me when I visited the Brotherhood?'

The Accountant looked genuinely puzzled. 'No, of course not.'

'And you didn't try to turn me into plastic boots just now?'

'I admit that. I did try, but I'm glad I failed — I couldn't have lived with the knowledge that I'd murdered a man.'

'Gold dust!' retorted Denson rudely. 'In any case, the attempt, successful or not, proclaims your guilt of the Bizman's murder — why else should you try to kill me?'

'I was afraid. I knew you suspected me, and there's a lot of circumstantial evidence against me.'

'If you were really innocent, you'd have no need to worry,' replied the Tec. 'Your insurance company would have soon disposed of circumstantial evidence.'

'I have no accusation policy,' whispered Cluth. 'I cancelled all my policies to finance the Capella-Arcturus-Fomalhaut participation. I'm completely unprotected.'

'Not even sickness or accident?'

'Nothing.'

'You're a fool,' commented the Tec. 'But that's not my problem. I know you killed the Bizman, and there's enough evidence against you to reduce Ros Kernwell's guilt probability rating to below the conviction threshold.'

'I swear to you I did not kill the Bizman!' Cluth pleaded. 'But I can't prove it with no insurance and no ready credit.'

Denson shrugged. 'That's no concern of mine. You tried to frame Ros Kernwell. My job is to prevent her being wrongly convicted.'

⋆　⋆　⋆

The Tec left Cluth in the office. As he went out, he glanced back at the ashen-faced figure slumped in the chair, and felt a twinge of pity. He suppressed it irritably. That wretch killed the Bizman, left Ros to take the blame and tried to kill me, he thought. He deserves no pity.

Denson drove back to the shuttle port and caught the evening flight to Joy City, taking the cableway out to Lovers' Lie-Inn. This time Seelya was there waiting for him. She came forward, smiling, her body tantalisingly visible beneath a semitransparent gown. She sniffed.

'I know,' said Sarn. 'I smell of chemicals. I'll shower straight away.'

'I like the aroma of heavy organics,' replied Seelya. 'It stimulates my adrenalin.'

She put her arms round Denson's

neck, and pressed her body against him.

'Well I'm not going to dab creosote behind my ears just to turn you on!' asserted Denson.

Seelya giggled. 'I'm not sure those chemicals aren't affecting you too. Something has certainly raised your temperature. That's not all it's raised either!'

Slowly she removed one hand from his neck and let it slide down his body.

Sarn pulled away.

'You know quite well what's making me hot,' he said. 'It's you. First I'm going to have a shower and then I'll demonstrate just what effect you have on me.'

As the hot water trickled down his body, Denson reflected that the day had ended better than it had begun — but then it was always less painful going to bed than getting up, particularly if you were sharing a bed.

★   ★   ★

Later, as he lay beside the slumbering Seelya, the Tec found he couldn't sleep. I'm going soft, he thought. I've cracked the case, and I can get Ros off the hook. So why am I so dissatisfied?

Finally, he could deny the reason no longer — he believed Cluth's protestation of innocence, even though he didn't know why. Somehow the idea of Cluth's guilt didn't fit the crime. He remembered too that the Accountant's surprise at hearing of the other attempts on Denson's life hadn't seemed feigned.

Still, he thought savagely, what did it matter if Cluth was innocent of the Bizman's murder? It wasn't Denson's job to find the truth, only to prevent his client being convicted. Cluth's guilt or innocence was Cluth's problem. Besides, if the Accountant hadn't murdered Borrowitch, he'd very nearly succeeded in bumping off Denson. He deserved what was coming to him. What would that be, he wondered? Thirty years, perhaps, although it depended on the exact probability of guilt — the higher the probability, the longer the sentence. It couldn't be much less than thirty years, though — thirty years hard labour for one of the prison companies while he worked off the compensation the insurance company would have to pay the heirs of his victim.

The prison companies were tough — convicts worked, or they got no food, and only days worked counted towards the expiration of the sentence. If you were lazy or sick, a ten year sentence could take twice that long to pay off in real terms. What's more, Cluth obviously had no wealth left to pay off any part of his sentence. He would have to work it out in its entirety.

Denson sighed. It was no use pretending. He believed Cluth, and there was no way to get Ros Kernwell off if Cluth was not guilty of the Bizman's murder. He had to admit to himself that the only satisfactory way for him to clear a client was to find the real villain. Sometimes he wondered if he was really being fair to his clients. They paid him to clear them. Cluth was no client of his, yet he knew he was effectively going to try and clear him too.

Seelya murmured and opened one eye. 'I thought you were tired,' she said.

'I am, but I can't sleep.'

'Then you can't really be tired. You need more exercise.'

Her hand slid up his leg, and for a while he forgot about detection . . .

★ ★ ★

As they breakfasted next morning, Denson was thoughtful.

'I suppose we'll have to leave Joy City now that you've cracked the case,' Seelya broke into his reverie.

'I haven't cracked it,' replied the Tec.

'But you've enough evidence against Cluth to reduce Ros Kernwell's guilt rating to well below the threshold!' objected Seelya, astonished.

'Cluth didn't do it,' asserted Denson morosely.

'What's that got to do with it? Your job is to get Ros off. You're not some off-world policeman employed by a government. Your employer is your client.'

'I know. I've been over that argument again and again, but I must know the truth. I'm not interested in finding scapegoats — and that's all Cluth would be.'

'Is he going to pay you to get him off?'

'He's broke,' replied Denson flatly.

'You're a fool!' Seelya suddenly flared at him.

Denson looked at her and felt sad. This disagreement was the nearest thing they'd had to a row since they'd met, but he couldn't change the way he felt about things. He had to go on.

Suddenly Seelya melted. 'Well, if that's the way your mind works, I suppose that's that. At least it means we can stay on here, which, providing you stop looking at me so stonily, is all to the good.'

'Sorry,' said the Tec. 'I'm glad you understand.'

'I'm not sure I do, but I'll accept it. What are you going to do next?'

'I'll pay Pawl Momad another visit.'

Seelya stood up. She was wearing her night robe, or rather she had put it on to get up. The girl stretched languidly and it parted at the waist. 'Are you going out straight away?' she asked.

Denson's throat was dry. 'There's no time like the present,' he averred, rather weakly.

Seelya smiled. 'That could be said about a lot of things . . . '

14

Fantasy Fabrics

It was nearly noon when Tec Sarn
Denson eventually set off to consult Pawl
Momad. He picked his way through the
city, traversing the street of the Get Rich
Quick studios, where the ever-hopeful
flocked to learn how to paint or sculpt a
masterpiece that could go straight into a
bank vault and confer unlimited wealth
upon them. Denson wondered how so
many could be so gullible. If the teachers
were capable of passing such a gift on to
their pupils, would they not themselves
already be so rich as to have no need to
teach?

Some of them professed to be so,
indeed, and claimed to instruct only as a
great favour to the multitude, or from
pure dedication to the dissemination of
art. Others made no such pretence, but
would-be artists flocked to their schools.

The Tec could only suppose that those who came believed they had some special genius or flair which would show itself in works far surpassing the mere craftsmanship of the instructors, once they had learned the mechanics of their chosen medium.

Whatever the reason, they came — painters, sculptors, writers, dramatists, novelists, poets, musicians, composers, dancers, actors, even illusionists. All came, some again and again, lured by the thought of striking it rich, just as the pre-collapse prospectors had been enticed hither by the expectation of gold. Despite the assiduous activity of the studios, there was no sign of a great flood of art to undermine the present regime.

Denson broke his irrelevant reverie — irrelevant, that is, to the problem of the Bizman's death. If he discounted Cluth, as he now felt he must, did that mean that the motive for the murder had nothing to do with the substitution of the fake pictures in the Bizman's account? It was possible that someone else had discovered the deception, but that would surely have led to a blackmail rather than murder — except if that someone had been Thirlward Meeran.

The Borrowitch fraud could conceivably lead to Bizman Meeran's ruin. Could Meeran have murdered Borrowitch out of revenge? It seemed unlikely. Had he been in Meeran's position, Denson would have been inclined to let Borrowitch know that he was rumbled, and give him time to put things right.

★ ★ ★

Pawl Momad seemed pleased to see Denson — probably thinking of the fee, reflected Denson sourly.

'I've got something for you!' declared the Joy City Tec, rubbing his hands together. He toed a button and a screen lit up with a picture of Edlin Borrowitch entering a night-dive with a woman.

'Any idea who the decoration is?' enquired Momad.

'Yes,' grunted Denson. It was Nadya Lasolere.

'She looks worth questioning,' grinned Tec Momad.

'I'll think about it,' promised Sarn.

'Don't we all,' sighed Momad.

'Nothing else?' asked Denson.

Another picture flashed on the screen.

'Edlin's decorative bit enters Joy City with his widow,' captioned Momad.

'When was that taken?' yelped Denson.

'This morning.'

The Gold City Tec sank back in his seat, his brow furrowed. Although he'd probed both Adelin and Nadya about their political leanings, it had been more a way of needling them into answering other questions, not because he'd thought there was anything in it. He still didn't, although their coming together to Joy City was intriguing, especially in view of the apparent association between the Bizman and Nadya. He was uncertain what to make of that particular piece of intelligence.

'Where did Adelin and Nadya go?' he asked.

'To Fantasy Fabrics.'

'Any sign of Obert yet?'

'No, nothing. Wasn't he with Ros Kernwell?'

Denson shook his head. 'Try keeping an eye on the Temple of the Brotherhood. He may have taken refuge there.'

Momad nodded. 'And you?'

'Oh, I'll be around,' evaded Sarn. 'I'll call you from time to time.'

★ ★ ★

Tec Denson zig-zagged across the city towards the fashion sector. Normally unresponsive to the advertisements which glared and shrieked along the boulevards, his attention was nevertheless cued by the name 'Fantasy Fabrics'. The density of its advertising was increasing. Intriguingly dressed female forms lounged across the cableway, or glided alongside it, the three-dimensional projections amazingly realistic, apart from their larger than life size.

Fantasy Fabrics itself was located in an inverted pyramid, apparently balanced precariously on its apex, the exterior dazzling with fluorescent reds and greens.

The Tec picked up the entrance cable, which swooped upwards into a gloomy gash in the side of the building. From this dark tunnel he burst into a kaleidoscope of colour and music.

He berthed his car and stepped out on to a floor into which his feet sank with every step he took. Rapid progress past the daringly arrayed models was impossible. At last, however, he reached firmer ground. A girl came towards him, her cloak flowing behind her in the warm breeze which pervaded the interior, to reveal an exquisitely proportioned body clad in a skin-tight jump-suit. Denson wondered idly if the nipples pressing through the thin material were her own, or if they came with the suit.

The vision dazzled him with her smile and welcomed him in dulcet tones, enquiring the reason for his visit. The Tec explained that he wished to talk to S. Chandon about the death of Bizman Borrowitch. As he uttered the word 'death', a shadow passed across the beautiful face, and its radiance was dimmed, as if he had uttered a forbidden thought. He saw muscles move in her slim throat and knew she was communicating sub-vocally with someone. At length she smiled again.

'I'm sure Bizwoman Chandon would be delighted to see you. Please follow me.'

Sarn would have been quite happy to follow her all afternoon, so delightful was the sight of her walking before him, but the distance was short.

'Please take this lift to the top floor,' she said, 'and then follow the guide.'

The guide sphere led him down a brilliantly carpeted corridor to a golden door, which slid open as he approached. He stepped through into a large room with two walls and the ceiling completely transparent, giving a view of sky and city that was magnificent. In the centre of the room floated a table. He heard the sound of breathing and swung round. Along the corridor a litter came floating, upon which reclined an elderly woman, one hand resting lightly on a small instrumented console.

The Tec stepped hastily into the room and the litter followed. It came to a halt close to one of the windows, with the woman facing into the room so that her face was obscured by the contrast of the bright daylight behind her. Nevertheless, the fleeting glimpse the Tec had snatched as the woman had passed him had been sufficient to show that she was very old, so her voice came as a surprise — it was sweet and musical, like that of a young girl.

'I was saddened by Edlin's death. He may not have been the greatest of men, but he was a good Bizman.'

'Was he?' questioned Denson.

'What do you mean?'

'Didn't you know about his picture switching racket? Instant credit by stealing from his own account at one bank to open a new account at another, the fraud being covered by substitution of faked pictures.'

'Nonsense!' protested Shani Chandon. 'Such a crude ploy would never fool an art auditor.'

'The Bizman didn't expect it to. He was a good customer and knew a lot about banks and the way they operate. He counted on switching paintings back and forth whenever an audit was likely. Sooner or later the fraud would have been discovered, but the Bizman expected his new export venture to realise its potential soon enough for him to escape detection. Perhaps he'd have been lucky — if someone hadn't killed him. Then, of course, the banks at which he had deposits conducted an immediate audit and Edlin's crime was uncovered.'

'How do you know all this? Or is it just supposition?'

'His confederate has confessed.'

'And who was this accomplice?'

'I prefer to keep confidences if I can,' parried the Tec.

'I suppose you think this will encourage me to unburden myself to you?'

'I'd be grateful if you could tell me something about the Borrowitch family.'

'I too am reluctant to betray confidences.'

'Would you be happy to know that Edlin's killer has escaped justice?'

'That depends on who the murderer was.'

Denson felt a slight sense of shock at this remark, and was irritated with himself for doing so. He reminded himself that justice was an intangible and abstract quality. It was the pursuit of justice — moral justice, economic justice, political justice — that had resulted in the imposition of so many tyrannies throughout the inhabited worlds. Governments paid lip service to justice, policemen and judges operated in its name — but not on Dorado.

Dorado's society despised abstract concepts — punishment for moral transgression was inapplicable. Crime was an economic evil, and the criminal must be made to restore the status quo as far as possible. Where robbery was the crime, it was a simple equation to solve — the value of the articles stolen, if not the articles themselves, must be recovered. If the malefactor was unable to pay, he must work off the debt — and accumulating interest — by labouring for one of the prison companies.

He reminded himself that the law machines did not dispense justice. They merely calculated the probability that an accused person was guilty of the crime.

With murder and other crimes of violence, it was more difficult to assess the cost of the crime, but very often it was set at the value of the life insurance policy payable by the victim's insurance company. In theory, a rich man might murder any number of the poor with impunity: they would be unlikely to have either a death investigation or death benefit policies of any great value. In practice, however, it was much more likely that a rich man would have the motive to murder another wealthy citizen than a poor man.

'I surprised you,' Shani Chandon's comment cut through his introspection. 'I don't see why you should appear so shocked.'

'Was the Bizman a good man in your estimation?'

'There are many people I liked better than the Bizman. If any of them murdered Borrowitch, I hope they get away with it. Why should I desire to lose two friends rather than only one?'

'But surely it is reprehensible to slay a good man?'

'I didn't say he was good,' corrected Shani Chandon. 'Not at any rate in the sense of virtuous. He was a reliable colleague — at least, I had thought him so. If what you say about his credit raising scheme is true, I shall have to revise my opinions on that score. As for morality — well, I've never troubled myself much about that, but perhaps Edlin was not a good example. I sometimes thought that he collaborated with me because it brought him into contact with so many young women who would be flattered by the attention of a successful Bizman.'

'Was his wife a customer of yours?' enquired Denson softly.

'Adelin? Oh yes. In fact she's here now with Nadya Lasolere. They intend to mourn Edlin in style, and are anxious to get the most exclusive clothes for the occasion — that means Fantasy Fabrics.'

'I wasn't aware you purveyed mourning clothes,' said the Tec. 'I'd always associated your fashion house with more exotic, not to say erotic, clothing.'

'There's no reason why a woman shouldn't look attractive when mourning!' retorted Shani Chandon.

'In view of what you said about Edlin's eye for the girls, I assume he wasn't normally accompanied by his wife on his visits to Joy City.'

'No, not usually. Although there was a time when he and Nadya came here together quite frequently.' She was leaning forward on her raft and speaking in a confidential whisper.

'You don't seem very surprised,' she said, disappointedly sitting back. 'Did you know about Edlin and Nadya? You must have done, otherwise you'd have been as shocked as you were about those other trifling matters.'

She yawned. 'I grow weary. Come and see me again some time. It's been amusing to talk to someone who still believes in morality.'

'One more question,' put in the Tec hastily. 'Did Ros Kernwell ever come here with Edlin?'

The old woman shook her head, and Denson sensed rather than saw her eyelids droop over tired eyes. He rose noiselessly and slipped from the room, then he returned to the Pawl Momad agency.

★ ★ ★

'You were right,' the Joy City Tec greeted him. 'My man had been outside the Temple no more than an hour when he spotted Obert coming out of the visitors' lodge.'

'What did your man do?'

'He put the frighteners on Obert to such good effect that the lad made no bones about coming straight back here with him. He's in the next room.'

★ ★ ★

Sarn Denson stared intently at Obert Borrowitch. The latter was nervous, but mustered sufficient courage to meet the Tec's scrutiny without actually flinching. He was a paler version of Jaimi, but his

251

face was less petulant.

'Why did you run away?' asked Denson suddenly.

'I didn't — that is, what if I did?' replied Obert.

'You didn't run away ... ' mused Denson. 'Then why did you come to Joy City? To look for Ros Kernwell, I suppose?'

Obert flushed, and no answer was necessary.

'You haven't found her,' stated the Tec. Obert remained mute.

'I know you haven't,' Sarn went on, 'because I know where she is.'

Obert started at this.

'Do you think she killed your father?' asked Denson.

'No, of course not!' replied Obert indignantly.

'Do you love her?'

'That's none of your business.'

'What will you do with the money you inherited from your father?'

Borrowitch was silent. Denson sighed. He played his trump.

'If you co-operate with me and answer

my questions, then I'll tell you where Ros is. I'm only trying to discover your father's murderer, and I am doing it for Ros, after all.'

'What do you mean, you're doing it for Ros?' demanded Obert.

'Ros retained me to reduce her guilt probability.'

'You're not from City Investigators?'

'Do I look like one of their half-baked operatives?' protested Denson.

Obert smiled. 'I'll trust you,' he decided.

A push-over, thought the Tec. Obert could never succeed the Bizman, whatever the latter had hoped.

'What will you do with your inheritance?' repeated Denson.

'Marry Ros, and help people,' replied Obert without hesitation. 'If she'll have me, that is.'

'What do you mean 'help people'?'

'Like the Brotherhood does. I'd go round the city seeking out people in trouble and help them to straighten things out.'

'Give them credit?'

'If that was what was needed, yes.'

'Your father wouldn't have approved.'

'He was a fine man in some ways, but he had his blind spots.'

'What about the exocities? That's where people go when they're really creditless.'

'I . . . I think I might do more good by preventing people from getting that desperate.'

'You're afraid of the exocity slums?'

'I've never been to one, but I've heard fearful stories. I don't think I'm the right sort of person to tackle them. Someone much tougher is needed — or a saint.'

'The Brotherhood of Earth goes to those places.'

'I know, and I admire them greatly for it, but I don't have their courage.'

'You want to enjoy do-gooding, and to enjoy it you need to stay alive, is that it?' sneered Denson.

'I know my limitations,' replied Obert quietly. 'I just couldn't cope with the degradation and danger that exists in the Heaps.'

'That's why you couldn't find Ros,'

observed the Tec acidly.

'What do you mean?' cried Obert.

'Ros fled to the Hives.' He watched Borrowitch closely, as the man struggled to overcome his fear; the fear of one who could always afford the sense of security that total insurance offers, suddenly confronted with the loss of protection.

'You can take me to her?'

'I can,' affirmed Denson.

'Then I will come. We'll bring her back to . . . back to safety.'

Sarn smiled suddenly. 'I think you might do for Ros after all,' he observed.

'What do you mean?'

'A lesser man would have said 'bring her back here', would have offered me money to risk my life to bring her out. You didn't. I guess you really do love her, and you've got more courage than you give yourself credit for. However, you don't have to put it to the test. She's no longer in the exocity, she's back here in Joy City. Here's her address.'

Denson handed Obert a plastic disc.

'Tell me, did you ever consider giving your inheritance to the Brotherhood?'

'Yes I did. In fact, if Ros won't marry me I shall probably join the Brotherhood and assign it to them.'

'Do the Brothers know this?'

'Oh yes.'

'I don't suppose they might have had your father assassinated and the blame cast upon Ros to get their hands on the credit?'

Obert regarded him aghast. 'You can't be serious . . . ' he whispered.

'No,' admitted the Tec. 'It's a ridiculous idea. Well, you'd better go and see Ros. Make sure she stays where she is for the time being, and don't draw attention to her.'

'Thanks,' acknowledged Obert. 'And thanks for going into the Heaps after her.'

'It's only what I'm paid for,' mumbled Denson. 'At least, I hope I'll get paid for it.'

★   ★   ★

When Obert had left, Sarn Denson asked Pawl Momad to ensure that he wasn't tailed, then he slumped down in a chair, brooding. He couldn't see any of the people he'd interviewed in the role of murderer, but perhaps he just lacked imagination?

For the umpteenth time, he told himself he was too easy going to be a Tec. He found it too difficult to believe ill of others, yet there were crimes committed, so there must be criminals. He had no idea what to do next. He supposed he'd just have to plug on until something turned up. Perhaps he should seek out Nadya Lasolere again, and confront her with what he'd discovered about her relationship with the dead man?

It was about the only lead he had.

15

Doubts

Tec Sarn Denson returned to Fantasy Fabrics. He came to a desk, behind which sat a dark-skinned beauty whose golden hair cascaded like sunshine on to the black night of her ebony shoulders.

'S. Chandon is still sleeping?' the Tec began formally.

The girl nodded.

'I arranged to meet Nadya Lasolere here,' Denson went on, 'but I seem to have missed her. Can you tell me her whereabouts?'

'Certainly.' The girl consulted a screen in front of her, upon which was listed the location of all people in the building as monitored by electronic eyes distributed throughout the complex, and linked to an individual recognition bank.

'She's in the swim room.'

Denson thanked her, and was rewarded

with a flash of gleaming white teeth. He walked down the corridor to the elevator rank, and entered one of the glass cylinders. He keyed 'swim room' into the control panel, and the capsule fell silently into the depths of the building. Its descent complete, it moved smoothly in a horizontal direction along a blue passage, until it stopped abruptly. The opening reappeared in the cylinder wall, and the Tec stepped through into a vast room. He knew it must be a chamber of some sort, although it gave the illusion of being out of doors.

A beach of golden sand stretched away in two directions, seemingly without end. Behind him were café terraces, and beyond them quaint buildings in the style of Old Earth. The sound of breakers was soft and soporific, and he could see the waves of the sea tumbling on to the beach in a swirl of white foam.

Above the ocean, which stretched away to the horizon, the sky was blue, and at the zenith blazed the sun now called Alpha Sol. Below it and to the left burned a bright daytime star, Beta Sol, formerly the planet Jupiter.

Palm trees grew in clumps along the strand, and in their shade lounged beautiful women, clad in all manner of beach wear. Denson would have bet a Matisse this had been Edlin Borrowitch's favourite haunt on his visits to Fantasy Fabrics.

The Tec strolled across the strand, admiring a lithe female who lay stretched out in the artificial sunshine, a tiny triangle of cloth bulging between her thighs, her breasts bare, but painted with two golden flowers centred on her nipples. She smiled at Denson, and turned over. He wondered how the fabric that adorned her front could possibly be kept in place.

Reluctantly he moved on, passing a group of girls in long transparent robes. The vista of the beach seemed to expand before him, but then he spied Nadya. He was pleased to see that Adelin was not with her.

'Hi,' called Sarn, and Nadya Lasolere swung round with an expression of displeasure on her face.

'Looking for a black bikini?' suggested the Tec. 'As part of the mourning outfit, I mean. I saw a nice one back there; at least I think it was a bikini — the girl seemed to have mislaid the top.'

'Adelin is buying her mourning clothes,' replied Nadya icily. 'I am not at all grieved at Borrowitch's death, and have no intention of displaying grief that I don't feel.'

'Should you be saying that to me?' asked the Tec. 'I'm still on the lookout for a murderer, after all.'

'You're a fool,' replied Nadya irritably, 'but I don't find fools amusing.'

Denson's manner changed.

'I'm sorry,' he said. 'I guess I'm just acting that way because I'm stymied. I can't get a lead anywhere. I know Ros is innocent — feel it in my bones — but I can't finger anyone else. I thought I had Cluth cold, but it wasn't him. I could get a good rating against him, enough to get Ros off and him convicted in the bargain, but it wasn't him.'

'Does that bother you?'

The Tec sighed. 'Yes it does. Stupid, isn't it? I guess I'm too soft to be a Tec.'

Nadya Lasolere looked at him thoughtfully. At length she said: 'If I could help you, I think I would, but there's nothing I can tell you that would be of any use.'

'I suppose you're right. Maybe I could talk to you about the case, though. It sometimes helps to talk it through. Let's get a drink over there.'

A little reluctantly, Nadya followed Sarn Denson to a café set on the terrace above the artificial beach. They sat at a table, and a girl came over to them. She smiled down at Denson, as she stood with her legs slightly apart, her navel at the level of his eyes.

'I'll have a Beteljuice,' Nadya prompted him gently.

'Oh, yes, same for me please,' ordered the Tec, telling himself irritably that if he couldn't keep his eyes off the women and his mind on the job, he'd soon be a pauper domiciled in an exocity.

'You had an affair with Edlin Borrowitch,' said Denson gently. It was not the approach he'd planned. He thought he'd spring it on her suddenly, brutally, to surprise and confuse her. Now he felt almost apologetic about mentioning it. That he did so immediately and without warning was not from intent to agitate, but simply to get it out of the way as kindly as possible. Nadya seemed to sense his feeling, and responded in the same manner.

'Yes I did.'

'Why? I should have thought you'd nothing in common. Your political views are diametrically opposed. You're a friend to Adelin. Why did you betray that friendship for a man you could never have liked?'

'It isn't entirely true that I didn't like him — at least, I think I felt sorry for him. Yes, partly I felt pity for him, and partly I was fascinated by him. I couldn't understand what made him tick — what was his life for? What satisfaction was there in it? For him — for anyone? He wanted me. I don't know why.'

'Perhaps he resented the influence you had with his wife. Perhaps he sought to dominate you in order to neutralise that influence.'

'That sounds a bit screwball to me.

Anyhow, he wanted me. I was interested in him. It didn't last long.'

'Did he ditch you, or did you ditch him?'

'Are these questions relevant to your investigation? Anyway, I thought you were going to try ideas out on me, to help you think, not to interrogate me.'

'Sorry.'

'Well, I don't much care anyway. He threw me over.'

'Did you find out about him, about what he got out of life?'

'No. Nor what he put in. I mean, what use was his life?'

'He created Borrowitch Textiles.'

'And what use is that?'

'It gave others work,' suggested Denson.

'Is that enough?'

'Without men and women like the Bizman, the system would collapse.'

'Would that be a bad thing?'

The Tec recalled his thoughts on the life of a worker in the textiles complex, and felt unsure of the truth, but aloud he said:

'Of course, you have those revolutionary ideas about government. Well, what have *you* ever achieved? At least Borrow-itch was a success in his own frame of reference — as a Bizman in the commercial world. As a revolutionary, how successful is your life?'

Nadya Lasolere went white. Was it fury, or had she a guilty secret? Could she have murdered the Bizman after all, as a revolutionary act? The Tec dismissed the idea as soon as it occurred — and yet he was puzzled.

'Tell me, you live very well without appearing to do very much. Was that another of Borrowitch's dubious accomplishments — to support you?'

Nadya's pallor was transformed by a violent flush.

'That's unnecessarily offensive!' she flared. 'You really are odious. If you want to delve into how people earn a living, why don't you start with that fancy piece of yours, Seelya Koto?'

Denson stared at her, uncomprehending.

'Hasn't it ever occurred to you to wonder how she gets by?' demanded Nadya. 'At the moment, I take it she's living off you.'

'What do you know about it?'

'I know you and S. Koto are living together.'

Denson didn't trouble to conceal his dismay. 'How on Old Earth did you find that out?'

Nadya smirked. 'Not so smart are you, Tec Denson? If it interests you, Petronelle Gradski told me. She . . . '

'Seelya Koto doesn't come into this at all!' broke in the Tec harshly. 'My only interest in your financial status is in relation to the Bizman's murder.'

Nadya Lasolere rose. 'For a while I'd begun to think there might be a decent human being behind that Tec façade, but now I see it isn't a façade. You're nasty and suspicious through and through. I hope we never meet again.'

The girl turned on her heel and stalked away, and the Tec sat staring after her. He tried to concentrate on reviewing the Borrowitch case, but he found his mind returning to Nadya's question about Seelya. He knew Seelya wasn't living off him, not in a complete sense. She seemed to have plenty of money of her own.

Perhaps she had inherited wealth. That certainly seemed the most likely explanation. How had Petronelle known about him and Seelya anyway? He couldn't remember mentioning it.

Deep in thought, Denson left the beach-wear department of Fantasy Fabrics. The trouble was, he reflected, he had either too many suspects or none at all. Try as he might, he could not assign a high guilt probability to any of the people involved in the case, but none of them had a probability that approached zero.

He found himself wondering again about Seelya. Curse that Lasolere woman, he thought. She's conjured up all sorts of doubts.

When he found himself distracted from his analysis a third time, he decided that he'd better scotch the doubts once and for all by finding out just what Seelya did do for a living.

Sarn Denson shied away from asking Seelya outright — not because he thought she wouldn't be straight with him, but because he feared the implication of mistrust it would carry. It was best, he thought, to make some discreet enquiries.

He took the shuttle back to Gold City and made his way to the information arcade.

⋆ ⋆ ⋆

Seated in the terminal room of Biography Incorporated, Denson scribbled his requirements on the screen with a light pencil. He preferred the rather old fashioned visual display to the voice simulators he could hear droning from other compartments. Although he knew nobody outside the cubicle could distinguish the spoken word, he had the irrational feeling that the silence of the screen was more confidential.

He felt almost guilty as Seelya's file began to unfold in glowing green letters. There wasn't much of it — in terms of Biography Incorporated, Seelya Koto was not an important person, even if she had become so to Sarn Denson. He felt a faint stab of uneasiness as he saw that she had formerly been a model at Fantasy Fabrics. A coincidence, he told himself, nothing more than that.

Seelya was beautiful, no one could deny that, least of all himself, and Fantasy Fabrics was renowned for using the loveliest girls to model its fashions. What could be more natural than Seelya having sought employment there? It was odd she hadn't mentioned it to him when he'd told her of his interview with Petronelle Gradski, but there could have been a million reasons why she didn't.

The file told him little else. She had abruptly stopped working for Fantasy Fabrics, and there was no record of a subsequent occupation.

Denson couldn't bring himself to consult the files of Gossip Associates. So much of the material contained in their files was totally unreliable, yet it could poison nonetheless. Instead he returned to Joy City and Fantasy Fabrics.

★　★　★

Shani Chandon had woken refreshed from her nap, and had consented to see him again. She was in a playful mood.

'Ah, the innocent returns! You don't

269

look very well. Perhaps detection doesn't really agree with you. Maybe you should take up modelling. We occasionally have a need for somebody plain to emphasise that we cater for the less beautiful as well as the birds of paradise.'

'Thank you,' replied the Tec absently, as he sought a way to raise the subject uppermost in his mind. In desperation, he launched into a repetition of his previous enquiries about Edlin.

'I believe you said he was friendly with quite a number of your girls,' he said at length. Shani Chandon nodded.

'Any in particular?' asked Denson. Shani Chandon reeled off a string of names, to which the Tec paid scant attention. Finally, he broached his real concern:

'I believe a girl called Seelya Koto once worked here?'

Shani Chandon watched him with eyes that were uncomfortably percipient. 'I believe she did. Yes, I remember her. She was a particular friend of Petronelle Gradski.'

A coldness seized Sarn's heart.

'Is she still employed by you?' he asked.

The old woman shook her head. 'I don't know what she's doing now. She stopped seeking assignments here soon after she took up with P. Gradski.'

★　★　★

When Denson had left, Shani Chandon called up Joy City Gossip. She filed the possibility that Tec Sarn Denson and Model Seelya Koto were closely involved, and then sat back to wait. Before long, her screen filled with a message from the gossip company:

Check of tip indicates high probability. The normal fee for this type of information will be credited to your account — see payment schedule available on request.

Every little helps, thought Shani Chandon, but it wasn't the credit she was interested in, it was the confirmation that her guess about the Tec's concern for Seelya Koto had been correct. Shani Chandon liked to know about these things. Herself immune, at long last, to the tyranny of the heart, it amused her to see its effects on others.

*   *   *

Sarn Denson sat in a small refreshment module on Play Street, a cup of coffee cooling in front of him. The characteristic fragrance of the blend from Sigma Draconis Five tempted his nostrils, but his brain was preoccupied. He had begun with self-pity and proceeded through intermediate stages to a numbed resignation.

Instinct urged him to abandon prying into Seelya Koto's past, to accept her present and all she offered him. Yet his years of detective experience could not easily be set aside. He knew there was something mysterious about her; knew that he would worry about it until it was cleared up. She was involved in some way with the Borrowitch tragedy.

*   *   *

His hunch was too strong to be ignored. He must press on with the investigation.

Denson put a call through to Jaimi Borrowitch in Gold City. The dissolute features of the Bizman's son glowed into life on the screen in the refreshment module's communication booth.

'What do you want?' he scowled at the Tec.

'I've been to see Petronelle Gradski.'

Jaimi's face showed interest. 'Some woman, eh?'

'You certainly know how to pick 'em!' responded the Tec equably.

Jaimi smirked in a particularly revolting fashion.

'How does she compare with your new girl?' went on Denson conversationally.

The youth tensed visibly. 'I'm not seeing anyone,' he replied evasively.

'But you have been.'

'So?'

'And you will again, no doubt, once the matter of your father's death is settled, and his estate can be divided up.'

'Oh sure,' muttered Jaimi.

Denson had copied a picture of Seelya from the Biography Incorporated files. Now he held it up.

'This your new girl?' he enquired casually.

Jaimi went white. 'What are you after?' he shrilled.

The Tec began to feel sick. He gritted his teeth and pressed on: 'She was giving you a good time, and you were feeding her credit, I suppose?'

'Get lost!' snarled Borrowitch. Denson almost wished the young man would break the connection, but Jaimi seemed a victim of both fear and fascination.

'She soon dropped you when your money ran out, didn't she?' sneered Sarn. 'You've seen the last of her.'

'That's what you think, Tec Know-all!' shouted Jaimi, goaded into losing his temper by Denson's denigration.

'That's what I know,' stated Denson firmly.

'Then why did she marry me?!' screamed Jaimi.

It was Denson's turn to go pale. The sickness in his stomach became a burning nausea in his mouth.

16

The Policy-Writer

Sarn Denson made his way to the apartment in which Ros Kernwell was hiding out. As he threaded his way through the city traffic, he concentrated wholly on his driving, his mind blank and cold.

Ros was pleased to see him. The time weighed heavily while she must remain immured. The Tec had cautioned Obert not to visit her or communicate with her in any way, except for that one initial contact, lest he be under surveillance by City Investigators.

Denson sank heavily on to a couch. The girl's pleasure evaporated as she sensed the Tec's mood of depression.

'What's wrong?' she asked anxiously. 'Do things still look black for me?'

Sarn sighed. 'No,' he replied, 'not for you. I think you're in the clear now.'

'That's wonderful! You know who did it — who killed Edlin?'

'I do,' replied the Tec, 'and I know why.'

'Who was it?' asked Ros.

'It would be best for you not to know. We have to play the next move very carefully, otherwise you'll get left with an expensive bill to pick up.'

'Yes, I understand that,' Ros nodded. 'If you go to City Investigators and tell them who the murderer is, they'll just accept the information and go after him. They won't have charged me, and so my accusation policy won't be invoked, and I'll have to pay for the investigation myself.'

'Exactly. Now that I can provide a highly probably alternative to you as the culprit, we need City Investigators to pick you up. So stay here and continue just as you have been, in hiding. I'll arrange for City Investigators to be tipped off, and they'll come and get you. It probably won't be a very pleasant experience, but you'll cope with it, and it won't last long.'

Ros shivered. 'I wish there was some other way. Can't you think of something?'

'No I can't!' snapped Denson, the

strain showing through again. 'There's nothing to worry about. A day or two more and this whole business will be over — for you, at least.'

And just starting for someone else, he thought.

★   ★   ★

Leaving Ros Kernwell, he returned to the Lovers' Lie-Inn. Seelya Koto was lying on the couch by the sun window, her eyes closed, her lithe brown body relaxed. He watched her nipples rise and fall as she breathed gently, and his gaze wandered along the bare body to her thighs, where the one scrap of clothing she wore seemed insecurely fastened. He moved into the room and she opened her eyes, and smiled at him.

'Good day?' she asked.

'So-so,' grunted the Tec.

She rose in one sinuous movement and came over to him. She put her arms around his neck and laid her head on his chest. He could smell the perfume of Altair, and feel the warmth of her body through his own clothing, but it did nothing to alleviate the chill around his heart. As if having a will of their own, his hands slid gently down her back and she shivered with anticipation. With an effort, the Tec controlled himself.

'I've been to see Ros,' he said abruptly.

'How is she?'

'Feeling the strain.'

'You never did tell me where you've hidden her,' remarked Seelya idly. 'I hope it's somewhere decent.'

It was the ideal opening, Denson realised, and realised too that the girl had plied him with a good many innocent enquiries in their few days together.

'She's in Sin Sector. A quiet boarding house called Rest-a-While,' he replied.

'Oh very respectable,' agreed Seelya. 'Odd really, that the one area of the city with such a disreputable sounding name should have become so staid.'

Sarn merely grunted. 'I'm afraid I must go out again,' he said.

'Must you?' pleaded Seelya. 'It seems so long since this morning. You won't be long, will you?'

'I don't know,' replied Denson, somewhat desperately. 'It depends on how things turn out.'

He gave the girl a swift kiss on the cheek, and almost ran for the door, leaving her staring after him with a puzzled frown on her face.

★   ★   ★

The Tec took his car and drove rapidly towards Sin Sector. He slowed as he crossed the sector boundary, and made his way to the Rest-a-While boarding house with more caution. He slipped into a vacant side wire, from which he could see the house — a low pylon crammed with small cheap modules — and settled down to wait. Denson pulled the hood of his jump-suit up over his face, and slumped down in his seat.

He hadn't long to wait before a big black cable car squealed to a halt before the Rest-a-While. Four men stepped out on to the reception balcony and entered the central column. A short while later, they re-emerged escorting Ros Kernwell, and re-entered the car, which trundled off up the street. No one but Denson appeared to have noticed the incident. Except for the lighted windows which showed here and there, the sole evidence of life in the street now that City Investigators had gone, were the tall weeds waving in the breeze below the cables, and Sarn himself, slumped in his small metal world.

Denson sat there for a long time, and he was full of bitterness, of self-reproach and self-pity. He thought of Seelya, of her beautiful body, her bright and infectious humour. For a time, he was almost tempted to go back to her, to warn her, to ask her to flee with him to Eta Cassiopeiae A or to Delta Pavonis. Duty — that duty his conscience proclaimed, not the ritual duty he owed to the Guild — restrained him; or was it habit? Was duty anything but the rule of habit? Denson could not say, but whatever this duty that bound him was, it was stronger than the love he felt for Seelya. Reluctantly, he bestirred himself, and activated the car. There was work to be done — fortunately. He drove swiftly to the Pawl Momad agency.

★ ★ ★

'Ros Kernwell's been taken in,' he told the Joy City Tec. 'She'll be charged. That means Aurum Life will have to assign her policy. I need to know to whom they assign it, faster than a cat can jump. Can you do it?'

Pawl Momad pursed his lips. 'Any clues?' he asked.

'It'll be a reputable firm,' decided Denson. 'Aurum underwrites so many clients that it has a high incidence of conflicting claims. If it assigned the secondary clients to poor companies, it would soon be losing policies because no one would want to risk being dumped. So they must use good lay-off brokers.'

'Here or in Gold City?'

Sarn shrugged. 'Gold City would be logical — that's where the crime occurred and where Ros Kernwell lives.'

'That's your home territory,' Momad

pointed out. 'Cheaper for you to sniff it out yourself.'

'Anything would be cheaper than your rates!' retorted Denson with a crooked grin. 'But I don't have much time. If I go there myself, it could be too late, and I don't have the facilities to conduct a long-range investigation.'

'All right,' Momad acquiesced. 'It's your client's money — or her insurance company's — or yours if you're out of luck.'

He got busy contacting agents and agencies in Gold City. Before long he had his answer.

'Consolidated Domestic and Commercial.'

'A good solid company,' mused Denson. 'Thanks. You've been a great help.'

He held out his thumb. 'If you've got the bill ready, I'll thumb-print it now in case I don't need to return.'

Pawl Momad pressed a button, and a transfer document slid out of a slot.

★　★　★

Denson felt depressed as the shuttle plummeted towards Gold City. Usually he enjoyed the occasional skirmish with the stuffy world of the big insurance companies, but today he had no stomach for it — nor for anything else.

From the shuttle port he took an omnicar to the offices of the Consolidated Domestic and Commercial Insurance Company Unlimited, where he was confronted by a dried-up scrap of a man, all wrinkles and wisps of grey hair, whose voice sounded like the hiss of air escaping from a newly opened tomb.

Denson mustered as much brightness and vigour as he could. 'I want to see the policy-writer in charge of the Kernwell case.'

'Who are you?' whispered the dried old husk behind the reception desk.

'Tec Denson.'

'I'll take your card and we'll call you if we need you.'

'You do need me,' answered the Tec flatly. 'I can save you a lot of time, and time means money.'

A vague uncertainty brought the promise of life after death to the dessicated features of the old man.

'I'll enquire,' he coughed.

He became a picture of inanimacy as he communicated sub-vocally with the policy-writer, then he stirred, like a pile of autumn leaves in the wind.

'Policy-writer Huxtable will see you,' he murmured. He raised a limp, almost transparent hand in a lifeless gesture, and a guide sphere floated down from the ceiling. Denson followed it until it reached the office of the policy-writer.

Huxtable was short and fat, and looked worried.

'Do sit down,' he invited. 'Now, as you said, time means money, so let's not beat about the buildings — you've got some information about the Kernwell case?'

'I can give you a case which will reduce the computer-estimated guilt probability to as near zero as a new-born babe's.'

'You have evidence?'

'Who needs evidence? The case against Accountant Kernwell is purely circumstantial. All that is needed to refute it is a better circumstantial case against someone else.'

The policy-writer nodded. He spread

his hands. 'Well, what's the story?'

'We must agree terms first,' Denson reminded him. 'Expenses and my fee.'

'Come now, Tec Denson, we're not employing you — we never employ lone operatives. If your hypothesis sounds as if it might be feasible, we'll make an ex-gratia payment.'

Denson leaned across the desk. 'Now see here, policy-writer, Ros Kernwell has a policy assigned to you. If necessary you'll use every Leonardo of that policy to try and clear her — your reputation would be shattered if you short-changed a client. I can save you some of that money — I'm not cheap, but I'm cheaper than the bigger agencies.'

Huxtable pursed his podgy lips. 'How much?'

'I know the yield of Ros Kernwell's accusation policy — I'll settle for half of it.'

The policy-writer hesitated. 'If my assessment of the strength of the case agrees with yours, we'll pay the sum you ask,' he said at length, 'but it's an all or nothing offer. We're not going to pay you to work up some half-hatched theory.'

'My hypothesis is complete,' replied the Tec quietly.

'All right,' sighed the policy-writer. His fingers danced lightly over the desk keyboard, and an agreement slid from a slot. He pressed his thumb on it, and the sensitive paper registered the imprint immediately. Denson did likewise. Huxtable left the sheet of paper between them, leaned back in his seat, and pressed another button. The ceiling changed colour, from a frigid blue to a more relaxing golden yellow, and the walls adjusted their own hue to blend with it.

'Now,' purred the policy-writer. 'What is your solution?'

Sarn gritted his teeth. Now that the moment had come to communicate his conviction to another, he experienced a revulsion at such treachery. It meant nothing that Seelya had betrayed him completely and systematically. He had known the warmth of her body; he retained the illusion that they had shared a bond of love. If it were his own freedom at stake, he would risk that rather than incriminate Seelya, but, despite his emotions, his sense of duty won through. He stated the facts as he saw them, his voice blank. The absence of any advocacy lent weight to his submission rather than detracted from it.

'Jaimi Borrowitch had two outstanding weaknesses — gambling and girls. He was able to indulge the latter principally as a result of his father's involvement with Fantasy Fabrics. It was there that he became acquainted with Petronelle Gradski. For a while he showered her with credit and attentions, but most of his credit went on gambling. P. Gradski felt it was a waste giving money to the saloon owners rather than spending it on her. She and Jaimi had a row, which led them to split up. Jaimi continued gambling in Gold City, but his father was well acquainted with his profligacy and took steps to limit Jaimi's income. Jaimi over-reached himself and defaulted on his debts, so that he was banned from the gambling scene.

'In the meantime, Petronelle Gradski had come to regret breaking with Jaimi

— she missed the additional income he had provided. She confided in a friend who was also a model from Fantasy Fabrics, Seelya Koto. Seelya suggested that she herself should try her luck with J. Borrowitch, and with that in mind came to Gold City. She soon struck up Jaimi's acquaintance, but was mortified that he could not afford to be as liberal as he had been before. She soon discovered, however, that he expected to receive large credits as one of his father's principal heirs, and she persuaded him to borrow on the strength of these expectations.'

'You have at least some evidence to back all this up?' interrupted the policy-writer.

'J. Borrowitch will testify to most of the facts about his relationships with the two women. The rest is reasonable supposition. There is a little additional corroboration. The affair between J. Borrowitch and P. Gradski was common knowledge in Joy City. When Seelya Koto came to Gold City, she brought with her a tape of Petronelle Gradski, which she gave to J. Borrowitch by way of

288

introducing herself.'

As he related what he knew must have happened, the Tec marvelled at the way his subconscious had rejected and frustrated his previous attempts to fit the facts to other hypotheses, and how everything had come together to form a pattern which he consciously wished to reject, yet could not in the face of this subconscious insistence.

'When Jaimi could no longer get credit, S. Koto cast around for a more permanent source of income. It was perhaps natural that the idea of Jaimi coming into his inheritance immediately should occur to her. If only the elder Borrowitch were to die, Jaimi would be rich and Seelya Koto could share in his wealth. It's a thought that must occur to countless men and women at some time or other — if only a particular person would die, all would be well. Is it a short step or a long one from wishing to scheming? Perhaps many feel the temptation to hasten the event. Most resist, but those few who succumb are potential murderers.'

'Never mind the philosophy,' interrupted Huxtable quietly. 'We're not paying for philosophy, just facts — or credible supposition, at any rate.'

Reluctantly Denson returned to his thesis.

'S. Koto persuaded J. Borrowitch to marry her, although I don't imagine much persuasion was needed. He was besotted with her, as doubtless other men have been. Once they were married, she set about plotting the murder of Edlin Borrowitch. Perhaps she conspired with P. Gradski — I certainly believe the latter knew after the event, if not before, since after I'd visited Petronelle, she warned someone that I was on the trail — that someone was Seelya Koto.

'Having access to the Borrowitch household, even if only secretly, S. Koto would have found an opportunity some-when to administer the poison to Borrowitch senior, probably by dosing his drink dispenser. He was very fussy about no one else using it. Once the deed was done, she took care to keep well away from the Borrowitch pylon, which piqued

Jaimi Borrowitch. I'm fairly sure he had no idea she was the murderer. He told her that he'd heard Ros Kernwell say she was going to employ a Tec to look after her interests, so S. Koto followed R. Kernwell and learnt that I had been engaged. She tampered with my car, probably while I was at the information centre.

'When I didn't return to my office, she assumed that her attempt to remove me had been successful. She tipped off Tec Garwen of City Investigators that Ros Kernwell had hired me, and that now I was missing presumed dead. It must have been quite a shock to her when I turned up again. She tailed me to the Golden Goose and there struck up an acquaintance with me, presumably with the object of finding out if I'd discovered anything which might endanger her. She can't have liked the way I was going about the investigation, as she tailed me when I set off to visit the Brotherhood of Earth, and ambushed me as I returned. When that failed, she tried a more subtle approach.

'My enquiries took me to Joy City and

she persuaded me to take her with me, partly I think to keep tabs on what I was doing, and partly because it gave her ample opportunity to try and undermine my confidence in my client. Once again she tipped off Garwen so that he was able to trail me into Joy, and she even hired a pair of professional discouragers to beat me up.'

'You must feel pretty sore about this woman,' commented the policy-writer.

'Feelings don't come into it,' returned Denson, but he knew it wasn't true. His emotions were so conflicting that they seemed to have neutralised each other.

'She also encouraged my investigation of Accountant Cluth. She'd nothing personal against Accountant Kernwell. As far as S. Koto was concerned, one scapegoat was as good as another.'

'And the picture fraud?'

'That was entirely Edlin Borrowitch's doing. If he hadn't been murdered, it would probably never have come to light.'

The Tec saw no profit in incriminating Cluth for his part in the fraud. He had no doubt that Borrowitch had been the instigator, and Denson's faith in natural justice, in right and wrong, was still reeling from his encounter with Seelya Koto's amorality.

Huxtable sat silent for a moment, and then pressed a button. The synthetic honey tones of a verbal computer filled the room:

'Preliminary assessment indicates the guilt probability rating for Model Seelya Koto is higher than that of Accountant Ros Kernwell, with respect to the murder of Edlin Borrowitch. Uncertainties arise mainly from the unsatisfactory explanation of the bank fraud.'

Cluth might have to be thrown in after all, thought the Tec.

'I think it'll do,' commented the policy-writer. 'Our programming is pretty well in line with that of the Justice Company computers, and I imagine that's where it will go to trial. The main problem, as I see it, is whether or not City Investigators have dug up any hard evidence against R. Kernwell.'

'It's most unlikely,' countered Denson. 'First of all, I don't believe for one moment she's guilty. Model Koto is almost certainly the culprit. So any evidence against Ros would have to be manufactured or totally fortuitous. City Investigators is a reputable outfit that doesn't go in for fake evidence. Secondly, if they'd have had any evidence, they would simply have arrested her in the first place — they wouldn't have goaded her into flight for self-incrimination if they could have nailed her otherwise. It wouldn't be good economics.'

Huxtable pressed the button again, and once more the treacly voice of the verbcomp filled the office:

'*That represents a crude approximation of the computed assessment of the situation.*'

Fuse you, thought Denson savagely. The whole cosy atmosphere was stifling him. They sat here warm and comfortable, discussing who was most likely to be sent to prison, as if they were at a restaurant choosing a meal.

'Well, I reckon you've earned the credit,' opined the policy-writer. 'We'll approach Model Koto as soon as possible. You don't know where she is at the moment?'

Sarn shook his head. It wasn't a lie, legalistically speaking, since the question had been imprecisely phrased. The Tec didn't know exactly where Seelya Koto would be at that moment. Nevertheless, he knew the policy-writer had been asking for her address, and that he did know. Still he kept quiet.

Huxtable sighed and leaned forward, picking up the agreement.

'The credit will be transferred to your account immediately,' he began.

But the constant repetition of the word 'credit', making him feel as if he had betrayed his lover for wealth rather than for duty, finally goaded Denson beyond endurance. He stood up and strode to the door, turning round only to snarl, 'Keep your credit. Just get Ros Kernwell off the hook, that's all.'

For the first time, the policy-writer showed an emotional reaction. He dropped back in his chair, an appalled and incredulous expression evident in his open mouth and popping eyes.

Denson left him there, and stalked off towards the exit.

17

The Girl Who Walked by Herself

Tec Sarn Denson sat in the pilot seat of his cruiser, high above the silver sea. He was far out over the ocean, and the city was no more than a golden line on the horizon, lurid in the setting sun.

He had been there a long time, hovering motionless above the restless waves. He was filled with self-pity and self-contempt. He was angry with himself for trusting Seelya, for allowing his emotions to cloud his judgement. He was sorry for himself because he had fallen in love with a woman who had betrayed him again and again. He despised himself for feeling as he did.

Even now, he could not bring himself to think harshly of Seelya, but instead felt anguish at what she must now suffer. Conviction could perhaps bring her thirty standard years as a prison company slave to work off the blood money insurance paid by Aurum Life to Edlin Borrowitch's family. Thirty years, that is, if she worked hard. Lack of enthusiasm for work amongst prisoners meant no food and an ever-increasing sentence. If she were rich, of course, she could buy off a part of her sentence, but she wouldn't have needed to murder the Bizman if she'd been rich.

Was it reasonable that a rich man could murder a poor man, knowing that the blood money insurance would be small, even if the investigation was enough to convict him? It certainly didn't seem just, but then what reason could a wealthy plutocrat have for murdering a creditless nobody? Probably none.

His thoughts returned to Seelya. It was possible that she might get off. The evidence against her was entirely circumstantial, and a clever defence might lower the guilt probability index sufficiently to achieve a non-proven verdict, or at least a reduced sentence. It wouldn't matter which of the law companies tried the case — they vied with one another for the reputation of greatest impartiality in order to attract litigants to their courts.

It was growing dark. Even at this distance, the lights of Gold City were becoming visible. Denson wondered if the agency hired by Consolidated Domestic and Commercial had located Seelya yet. It had been a futile gesture on his part to fling the fee back at them. They would credit it to his account anyway, if only to keep their books straight. The urge to know what was happening grew on him, but he did not relish contacting Huxtable for the news.

Almost uncomprehendingly, he reached out towards his communications console and punched out a call to the room he and Seelya had occupied at the Lovers' Lie-Inn. The screen glowed to life, and there she was smiling at him. All that he had endured since he left her might have been a dream.

'Where are you?' she asked. 'I was beginning to worry.'

Denson told her, and once he had begun, he went on to tell her what he had been doing, and how he had come to realise what she had done. Did he hope she might deny it? Or might be able to offer proof that she was not the murderer? He could not say. Was he so distraught at the thought of her in captivity, that he was compelled to warn her and give her a chance to escape? Perhaps. After all, it made no difference to Ros Kernwell's defence if Seelya Koto was not arrested and charged — indeed, it might strengthen the case if Seelya were to flee: a clear admission of guilt in the legal programming of the law machines.

As the purport of his message became clear to the girl, he saw sudden hatred flare in her beautiful violet eyes, hatred of him. Where he had imagined love, and found only self-interest, he now evoked hate. That was soon replaced by fear. His last doubts, so carefully preserved, vanished like a frail mist before the fierce sun. There could be no mistake — Seelya Koto was guilty, and now she sought a way of escape. Abruptly she broke the contact, and the Tec was left staring at the bright but blank screen. With leaden heart, he turned off the set.

Stars were beginning to challenge the

vanishing glare of the setting sun, and he stared out at them, his eyes drawn as ever to the faint fleck of Alpha Sol. How long he sat, he didn't notice, but he was startled from his melancholy by the insistent burr of the communications centre. He accepted the call, and an unfamiliar face swam up from the depths of the screen.

'Greetings, Tec Denson.' The formal tones steadied Denson's nerves. 'I am Tec Lim Pa of the Big Eye Agency. Consolidated Domestic and Commercial may have informed you that they had employed me to find Suspect Koto. No?'

Denson shook his head, saddened to hear that Seelya was no longer Model Koto, but Suspect Koto.

'We eventually found her refuge in Joy City, but she had gone.'

Denson's heart lifted slightly at this news. The Tec from Big Eye licked his lips. He seemed reluctant to continue.

'She had not been gone long, and we picked up a description of her car from a man who had been watching her comings and goings. We guessed she would head out of the city, and posted agents at all the intercity cableway toll booths.'

Denson nodded. It was the obvious thing to do if you had the manpower.

'We would have lost her, though, but for pure chance. One of our operatives heading for the West Coast Expressway spotted her car heading out towards the city boundary and gave chase. We picked up the report, and I cut across to intercept, since I was in the neighbourhood. She was heading for the exocity Sekcentexo.'

Fear clutched at Sarn. The exocity was no place for a girl by herself. Ros Kernwell had been lucky, very lucky, but it was not expected that Seelya Koto would be so fortunate. And she was making the attempt at night.

'The suspect halted her car on the boundary cableway, and jumped out. We prepared to follow.'

Lim Pa swallowed and licked his lips again.

'The moggies got her,' he rasped, shuddering, despite being the hardened Tec that he was. 'There was a scream of terror, and we saw the dark tide of cats flowing through No Man's Land. There was another scream — indescribable. Then there was silence.'

Denson stared at the screen, unable to take it in. As the full horror of what the other man was saying dawned on him, he broke out in a cold sweat. 'Was there nothing you could do?' he whispered.

Lim Pa shrugged. 'We fired our lasers into the horde, but we killed only a few. You need flame throwers to halt a moggy pack — and it happened so fast. From what I gather, there was no doubt she was guilty. By the time she was released, she'd have been an old woman. Perhaps she's better off dead.'

Sarn said nothing. He sat immobile. His silence made Tec Lim Pa feel uneasy.

'Are you all right?' he enquired. 'I hear you had some narrow escapes on this case. Maybe you need a rest.'

Denson stirred. 'Maybe,' he muttered, and broke the connection.

★ ★ ★

Outside the sky was dark and the stars gleamed mercilessly. Mechanically, Denson moved back to the cruiser's pilot seat and sank into it. The cruiser angled down towards the heaving deep, and hit the surface amidst a cloud of spray, phosphorescent in the moonlight.

With a surge of power, the boat leaped forward, thudding over the wave crests, out towards the endless ocean . . .

We do hope that you have enjoyed reading this large print book.

Did you know that all of our titles are available for purchase?

We publish a wide range of high quality large print books including:
Romances, Mysteries, Classics
General Fiction
Non Fiction and Westerns

Special interest titles available in large print are:
The Little Oxford Dictionary
Music Book, Song Book
Hymn Book, Service Book

Also available from us courtesy of Oxford University Press:
Young Readers' Dictionary
(large print edition)
Young Readers' Thesaurus
(large print edition)

For further information or a free brochure, please contact us at:
Ulverscroft Large Print Books Ltd.,
The Green, Bradgate Road, Anstey,
Leicester, LE7 7FU, England.
Tel: (00 44) **0116 236 4325**
Fax: (00 44) **0116 234 0205**

THE RESURRECTED MAN

E. C. Tubb

After abandoning his ship, space pilot Captain Baron dies in space, his body frozen and perfectly preserved. Five years later, doctors Le Maitre and Whitney, restore him to life using an experimental surgical technique. However, returning to Earth, Baron realises that now being legally dead, his only asset is the novelty of being a Resurrected Man. And, being ruthlessly exploited as such, he commits murder — but Inspector McMillan and his team discover that Baron is no longer quite human . . .

THE UNDEAD

John Glasby

On the lonely moor stood five ancient headstones, where a church pointed a spectral finger at the sky. There were those who'd been buried there for three centuries, people who had mingled with inexplicable things of the Dark. People like the de Ruys family, the last of whom had died three hundred years ago leaving the manor house deserted. Until Angela de Ruys came from America, claiming to be a descendant of the old family. Then the horror began . . .